THE SECRET OF THE BLOODSTONE NECKLACE

Susan M. Viemeister

ISBN-10: 1724358693
ISBN-13: 978-1724358691

Edited by Maggie Bradbury

CONTENTS

ACKNOWLEDGMENTS

Even though this is a work of fiction, I did use my house as inspiration for the house in the book. Since my house has its own ghosts, this led to some interesting happenings during the writing of this book, some of which even made it into the story.

Thanks Maggie for being such a trouper, even though my "techie spirits" were out in full force. Some things are just beyond our control.

CHAPTER ONE

Jolene Turner took in the scenery as she drove along. It was a clear, crisp Friday in October. *Friday the 13th*, she mused. She hoped that wasn't some sort of omen. Jolene had left New York before dawn, in an attempt to avoid the rush hour traffic. Despite driving for the last eight hours, she was calmed by the scenic countryside of Virginia. The rolling hills, with endless pastures of green grass dotted with cows, was such a change from all the concrete buildings and people in New York. She could feel the tension leaving her body as the miles clicked away. The more distance she put between herself and New York, and Garvin, the better.

Turning off the highway, Jolene drove along the quiet country roads, marveling at the nearly vacant highways. Occasionally, she would pass another vehicle, mostly pickup trucks. She smiled as she remembered encountering a farmer driving a tractor. *That was something you didn't see back home*, she thought to herself. "Back home? No. This is now my home," she said out loud. "I'm never going back there. This is where I want to be." A pang hit her chest as Jolene spoke out loud. She realized she was trying to convince herself that she made the right

Susan M. Viemeister

decision. Moving five hundred miles away, where she didn't know a soul, made Jolene a bit anxious. She was driving into the unknown. *Why am I doing this? Am I really so stupid to think Garvin can't track me down? What the hell was I thinking?* The calmness Jolene had been feeling began to fade. "I need to put it behind me. Concentrate on my new life," she said. Shaking her head, she took a big, calming breath of air, and focused once again on the scenery.

She soon found herself turning onto the gravel driveway of the ancient farmhouse she had purchased. The gravel crunched as she drove up the quarter mile driveway. The house sat on a small hill facing the field instead of the road. Following the driveway, she bypassed the front of the house. She continued around to the back, where it opened into a courtyard, surrounded by several barns. Jolene parked the car in front of a barn that had been converted to a garage, got out and stretched. She stood for a few moments, taking in the view. The house was a typical two-story farmhouse, with a wrap- around porch. It had been white at one time, with a black metal roof, but was in desperate need of paint. The grass and bushes around the house were overgrown, resembling a small jungle. The house had been abandoned by the previous owners, sitting empty for almost a year before Jolene bought it. She glanced around at the surrounding fields, all of which needed attention. The farm itself was forty acres, surrounded by other farms that were anywhere from fifty to over a hundred acres. She could only see the house across the road, set back on its own hill. There was another house about a half mile away on her left. She wanted space. Well, she got it. Now, standing here alone, she realized how isolated she would be.

"I guess I better get on with it."

Popping open the trunk of her car, Jolene unloaded her bags.

2

She hadn't brought much with her, choosing to sell, or give away the majority of her possessions prior to moving. She did have some furniture, like her bedroom suite, on the way. The moving van wouldn't arrive until the morning, so tonight she would have to rough it, sleeping in a sleeping bag. *It will be an adventure,* she thought to herself. *Like camping when I was a kid.*

"Poor house looks so sad. Even a bit spooky. Why was I so drawn to you? What happened that made your owners leave in such a hurry?" Jolene addressed the house. "Listen to me, I sound like one of my novels. House is abandoned by the owners, offered at such a low price some fool from New York buys it, thinking it will solve all her problems. Next thing you know, she finds out the place is haunted. Then all sorts of weird shit starts happening." Jolene gave a nervous laugh. "I've been on the road too long. I need a drink."

Gathering up her suitcases, she headed to the back door. She stepped up onto the porch and unlocked the door. Attempting to open it, she found the door was stuck. Muttering a curse, Jolene put her shoulder to the door, put her weight behind it and shoved. The door flew open, and she stumbled into the house.

"I guess that will be at the top of the repair list," she said. Picking up her bags, she brought them inside. She set them down and looked around. She was in what passed for a kitchen. It was tiny, though to be fair, her apartment in New York wasn't much bigger. The walls and moldings were bright yellow, causing her to shield her eyes. The cabinets were a nondescript oak, the floor was a mud colored linoleum, and the refrigerator was white, as was the stove.

"Hideous. I know what is getting renovated first." Jolene continued into the rest of the house. The kitchen led into a dark, dreary dining room. A door on the wall facing the front yard opened onto a small porch, where Jolene found a washer.

"Seriously? I don't remember seeing that when I viewed this place," she said, shaking her head in amazement. "But, come to think of it, I don't remember a laundry room either." With a sigh, she turned and walked through the doorway into the living room. On the wall facing her, was a closed-up fireplace. On the left of the fireplace was a narrow door. She opened it, finding a small closet. To the right of the fireplace, the wall extended out. She remembered this was a small bathroom. Jolene walked over to the bathroom, opening the door. There was a sink, shower and toilet, with barely enough room for her to turn around. She closed the bathroom door, pondering who put a bathroom in a living room. She walked through another doorway to the left of the fireplace into the hall. She turned to the right and faced the front door. A stairway on her left led up to the second level. The hallway was painted a deep, depressing orange. To her right was another room, which contained the main source of heat for the house, a wood burning stove.

Jolene walked up the stairs. They led to a small landing, then turned to the left with two more stairs, leading into a hallway that was open on one side overlooking the stairs. A railing prevented anyone from falling to the first floor. There were large windows on the wall facing the road and the other end of the hallway, creating quite a bit of light. At the top of the stairs, another short hallway led to a bedroom on the right. Straight ahead was another impossibly small bathroom. This one contained a sink with separate hot and cold water faucets, a toilet and a claw foot bathtub. Returning to the open hallway, she walked to the other bedroom at the end of the hall. She looked around, decided that would be her room, then returned downstairs.

The day was warm, the air in the house was stuffy, so Jolene opened the windows. A slight breeze blew through. She stood in front of one of the windows for several moments, taking in the view. She was startled by movement behind some of the bushes. Several deer stepped out, casually wandering across the overgrown front yard. Jolene smiled as she watched them, her sense of calm returning. The deer continued across the yard, then leapt over the worn out fence that divided the yard from the pastures, and bounded off. Jolene returned to the kitchen to get her bags. It was time to begin unpacking.

It was early evening by the time she finished unpacking and settled in. She ate a sandwich purchased at a run-down convenience store she had passed on the way down, hoping it had been made sometime during this century. Exhausted from the drive, she decided to take a hot bath and get some sleep. Tomorrow would be another long day. After making sure the doors were locked, she went upstairs to the bathroom. Anticipating a long, relaxing bath, she started the water. Taking off her clothes, she got in, and sank into the tub. She let the hot water soak away the stress of the day. Eventually, the water cooled, and Jolene realized she had nearly dozed off in the tub.

"That would have been interesting. Here one day and I fall asleep and drown," she laughed at herself. With a sigh, she pulled the drain plug, forlornly watching the water vanishing down the drain. Stepping out of the tub, she wrapped herself in a towel and headed for the bedroom. After drying herself off, she put on an old tee shirt and sweatpants, and crawled into the sleeping bag. Despite the accommodations, she was soon fast asleep.

It was the vibration in the floor that woke her. The house was built in 1901, and the floors upstairs flexed when walked on. When Jolene first looked at the house she found it disconcerting, but the real estate agent assured her it was normal for a house of this age, and that she wouldn't fall through the floor. Now, in her sleeping bag on the floor, she could feel movement, as if someone was walking in the room. Sitting up, she noticed the room was dimly lit by the farm light outside the window. Looking around, it was obvious no one was there. The vibration had stopped. Jolene was thinking she had imagined it when she felt a light breeze. Wide awake now, she scrambled out of the sleeping bag, running to the light switch. The light bulb in the ceiling was bright, blinding her for a moment before her eyes adjusted.

"What the hell?" she asked out loud. Walking to the windows, she checked that they were closed. The room was empty of any furnishings, it was just Jolene and her sleeping bag. Nervously, she walked to the hall. No one was there. Moving to the other bedroom, she looked for any signs of life. The other room was also empty.

"It's my over active imagination, I guess. If nothing else, it will make a good plot line for the next book," she said. Reluctantly, she crawled back in her sleeping bag, leaving the light on in the room. Not feeling or hearing anything else, she soon drifted off to sleep.

CHAPTER TWO

The sun streaming in the window woke Jolene. Between the long drive and sleeping on the floor, her entire body ached. Groaning, she crawled out of the sleeping bag and stood up. Feeling beat up and much older than her thirty-two years, she hobbled to the bathroom. After washing her face, she assessed herself in the mirror. Her short, auburn hair needed some serious attention. The layers stuck out at all angles, looking as if she stuck her finger in the light socket. Wetting her hands, she ran her fingers through her hair, until it was acceptable. Her dark brown eyes looked tired, but some much needed caffeine would fix that. All things considered, she didn't look too bad.

Returning to the bedroom, she noticed the light was still on. Turning it off, she pondered what had happened. Or, what she thought had happened. In the light of the day, it all seemed like a dream. *Maybe she had dreamed it,* she thought. *After all, it is an old house. Things are bound to creak and move. I'm just not used to it. Like the stairs.* Jolene noticed that several of the stairs creaked when you stepped on them. Convinced she was overreacting, she changed into a clean tee shirt and jeans, then made her way downstairs to the kitchen.

She searched her bags for the tea and sugar. Luckily, she thought to bring a tea kettle and coffee mug. While the water heated, she munched on a trail mix bar she had packed for the ride down. Having been in such a hurry to get here, she didn't think about the house not having any food. She also didn't bring much that would allow her to make anything to eat, but the movers would be here soon. Then she would go shopping. A girl couldn't live on trail mix bars, after all.

The air in the house was still a bit musty since the house had been closed up for so long. The day was forecast to be sunny and warm, so Jolene set about opening the windows in order to let the fresh air in.

That's better, she thought as a gentle breeze blew through the house.

Once her tea was ready, Jolene walked out the back door. After a moment, she sat on the step. It was a beautiful morning. The air was crisp, the sky lightening to a glorious blue. The leaves were turning stunning colors of red, yellow and orange. The landscape looked like a something from a magazine. *Maybe I should start painting again,* she thought. The spell was broken however, by the arrival of the moving van. Jolene got up, watching it struggle up the gravel driveway, before it stopped in front of the house. She walked over, standing at the back of the van. The men dropped the ramp, preparing to unload her belongings.

The men began by bringing in her bed. Jolene noticed that they were a lot more casual, and slower, than the movers in New York.

She followed the men as they struggled up the stairs with her bed. As they entered her bedroom, she noticed a couple of wasps flying around.

"Ugh. I hate bees!" Jolene looked around but couldn't find anything she could use to kill the wasps. Returning downstairs, she found a magazine in her bag and brought it back upstairs. Before she could do anything, she noticed not only were there more wasps, now, there were hornets.

"Oh my God. What the hell?" she asked.

The movers were just finishing setting up her bed. One of them looked around and noticed the hornets.

"You don't want to get stung by one of those," he told Jolene. "They go for your jugular. I have a friend that got stung by one of them, he still ain't right."

"Seriously? Where are they coming from?" Jolene looked around the room.

"These old houses are always full of bees," the other man told her. "I'll bet your attic is full of them. You don't see them while it's cold. Once it warms up, they all wake up."

"Wonderful," Jolene said.

The man smiled. "Welcome to the country. If I was you, I'd head over to the farm store in town and get yourself some spray. They'll know what kind you need."

"Thanks. I'll do that right away."

In short order, the few pieces of furniture were in the house, along with several boxes of odds and ends. She watched the van roll down the driveway, leaving a cloud of dust in its wake. Jolene wanted to unpack the boxes but the large number of wasps and hornets now flying all over the house changed things. She knew she had to go into town and get the bee spray. No way could she stay in a house filled with hornets.

Her stomach growled. She realized it was early afternoon, and she was starving. She would get something to eat in town and stop at the grocery store. Now that she had a couple of pots and pans, she could even stock the refrigerator. After a quick check in the mirror to be sure she was presentable, she grabbed her keys, and headed out the door.

Sitting in the small cafe, Jolene gazed around at the other people eating their lunch. A couple of older men dressed in camouflage sat at the counter. One man was telling a story that had the other man laughing. An older couple sat at a table, drinking coffee, and looking out the window. Another man, younger, wearing coveralls and work boots, sat at a table reading a newspaper. The rest of the place was empty. Jolene wished she had brought something to read. The looks she received when she walked in spoke volumes. This was a small town. She was a stranger. The men at the counter paid their bill, getting up to leave. They waved at the other people in the cafe. Clearly everyone knew everyone else. She, however, was an outsider.

Jolene avoided making eye contact with the men as they left, feeling self-conscious. *What would Garvin do?* She wondered. *He would walk in here like he owned the place. He would find out who the movers and shakers were in this town, if there were any, and buddy up to them. That is what Garvin would do. Then he would make some snarky comment about how timid she was.* Jolene didn't want to think about Garvin. Not after everything that had happened. He was in her past. She was here to start over.

"What can I get you, honey?"

Jolene jumped. The waitress had appeared out of nowhere. Waiting patiently, pen hovering over her pad, the waitress waited for Jolene to speak.

"Uh. I'll have the tuna salad please," she answered.

"Would you like that on white or wheat?"

"Wheat. And a coke please."

"Sure thing. You must be new in town. How long are y'all staying?" the waitress asked in a soft drawl.

"I just bought a house here," Jolene replied.

"Oh really? Where?"

"It's about ten miles south of here. On Crab Apple Road."

The waitress stared at Jolene for several moments. "What house did you buy? Not the old Overstreet place?"

"Actually, yes. That is the house. Do you know it?" Jolene asked.

"I better get your order in, honey. The food will be ready in just a little bit." Jolene watched as the waitress scurried back to the kitchen.

That was odd. She thought. Shrugging her shoulders, she glanced around in time to see the other diners suddenly avert their gazes. They had obviously been listening to the conversation. Jolene shivered. This place was beginning to creep her out. She wondered if she had been in too much of a hurry to leave New York. Maybe she should have done some research on the area. *Give it time. It's just culture shock. You're not in New York anymore. Once you get adjusted, it will be fine,* she told herself.

After lunch, Jolene located the farm supply store. She wandered the aisles filled with supplies for horses, cows, dogs and cats. There was even an aisle for rodent removal. She considered the traps, but decided to wait. The bees came first. Walking to the end of the aisle she found the bee spray. She picked out ten cans of spray, and along with the mouse traps, heading to the checkout.

The woman at the counter smiled when Jolene placed the spray on the counter.

"I see someone has a bee problem," she smiled at Jolene.

She appeared to be in her thirties, attractive, with her brown hair cut into a 1970's shag hairstyle.

"Yeah. The whole house is filled with them. I hate bees," Jolene told her.

"Well, this should take care of them," the woman laughed as she rang up the purchases.

"I sure hope so," Jolene smiled. "It's going to be a war on bees when I get home."

"Good luck," the woman smiled. "You must be new around here. I don't remember seeing you before."

"Yeah, I just moved here yesterday," Jolene replied.

"Well, glad to meet you. I'm Rhiannon," the woman held out her hand. Jolene stared at her, then smiled.

"Jolene." They shook hands, then started laughing.

"Let me guess, your momma was a Dolly Parton fan, " Rhiannon said.

"Yep. And yours was a Stevie Nicks fan." They laughed again. "What are the odds?" Jolene asked.

"For real," Rhiannon smiled.

"Hey, while I'm here. I'm looking for a contractor to do some work on my house. It's an old house and needs lots of work. Is there someone you would recommend?" asked Jolene.

"Oh, you need Lee. He's the best contractor around. He does real nice work and is extremely honest and reliable." Rhiannon wrote down a name and number on a piece of paper and handed it to Jolene.

"Thanks! I'll give him a call tonight," Jolene said.

"Where did you say you live?" asked Rhiannon.

"I bought a place on Crab Apple Road." Jolene noticed the change in the other woman's expression.

"Not the old Overstreet place?"

"Yes, that's the one. Why?" asked Jolene.

"Honey, y'all are gonna need more than bee spray with that place."

"What do you mean?" Jolene suddenly felt uneasy. Something was going on, and she wanted answers.

"Well, I shouldn't be spreading no stories. I'm sure it's a fine house. Don't you listen to me none," Rhiannon smiled. Another customer had come up behind them, and Jolene realized the conversation was over.

"Well, it was nice meeting you. Bye," Jolene said.

"You too, bye," Rhiannon responded.

Gathering up her purchases, Jolene left the store, well aware that both Rhiannon and the customer were watching her.

After leaving the farm supply store, she headed to the small grocery store where she loaded up the cart with supplies. She drove through the small town, trying to get her bearings. Main Street consisted of a couple of banks, the post office, courthouse, a few offices and a couple of fast food places. Oh, and the local newspaper. She also located the laundromat, the library, the sheriff's department and eventually, the hospital. Satisfied she could find her way around town, she headed home.

The country roads were, to Jolene, nerve wracking. They were winding, hilly, with no edges. Houses were few and far between, once she left the town. Open fields with cows grazing contentedly lined the roads. Jolene also noticed deer grazing in some of the fields. She would need to be on her toes in the event the deer decided to run in front of her car. She had both hands on the steering wheel, bravely driving 45 mph. Still, cars and trucks would suddenly be in her rearview mirror, riding her bumper. She passed a speed limit sign: 55mph.

"What are they crazy? How can you drive these roads that

fast?" she shouted, as yet another pickup truck passed her, the driver glaring at her as he flew by.

"I hope you crash, asshole!" she yelled after him. "Damn! And people say New Yorkers are bad drivers. These people are insane!"

Her hands were still gripping the steering wheel for dear life when she finally pulled in her driveway. Only then did she start to relax her grip. Cruising slowly up the driveway, she parked behind the house. She sat in the car for a few minutes, gathering her thoughts. The strange encounters in town had her rattled. She felt as though she was the butt of some joke that she didn't understand. It's just that everything is so different from what she was used to, it was almost like culture shock. People here had a different way of talking. It probably wasn't anything at all. She was reading far too much into the conversations. Most likely she was overreacting due to all the stress of the move. She would just need time to adjust. Then it would all make more sense.

Getting out, she unloaded the car, making several trips to bring in the groceries.

It was on her last trip that a car pulled up, parking behind her car. A middle-aged woman got out carrying a wicker hand basket and approached Jolene.

"Hi!" she called out brightly. "I'm Nancy. I am the welcoming committee. You must be Jolene." The woman extended her hand. Putting down her bag of groceries, Jolene shook the woman's hand.

"Hi. Nice to meet you," she said.

"Well here, this is for you," Nancy said, handing over the basket. "You'll find all sorts of information about our town in here. There are also lots of coupons from the stores and businesses. It's a great way for y'all to get to know where everything is." The woman glanced nervously at the house.

"Thank you. That's very nice. Would you like to come inside?" asked Jolene.

"Oh, no, no. Thank you, no. I really must be going. I, uh, just wanted to welcome you to the area. My card is in there if y'all ever need anything," Nancy answered hurriedly. "It was very nice meeting you. I hope to see you again. Bye!" Nancy slid into her car, backed up, and with a wave, quickly drove down the driveway.

Jolene stared after the car for several minutes. "These people are weird." After a moment she shrugged. She wasn't going to think about it anymore today. She had other things to take care of, like the bees. Picking up her grocery bag and the basket, she went inside the house.

Once she had everything put away, Jolene set about attacking the wasps and hornets with the spray. Soon, their dead bodies were everywhere. Satisfied she had killed them all, she cleaned up the remains and finally began unpacking her boxes.

CHAPTER THREE

"You know a lot of these old houses don't have closets. Back when they were built, folks used armoires and dressers to store their things. Course, it wasn't like they had an awful lot back then, either," Lee said as he and Jolene walked through the house. She had called Lee after she got home and he agreed to come out the next day.

Jolene had been taken aback when he first showed up. Lee was dressed in coveralls that did little to hide his fit body. He was a few years younger than she, with shaggy, light brown hair, blue eyes and a friendly smile. He looked like a rock star. Jolene was immediately drawn to him.

"It's funny, I never thought about closets before. It wasn't until I went to hang up my clothes that I realized there is only one small closet downstairs. None in the bedroom."

"Don't worry. I'll make some nice, big closets for you," smiled Lee. Jolene felt her heart skip a beat. *Damn, he's cute,* she thought.

"So, I'm thinking of putting one big closet in each bedroom, then one downstairs. Maybe in the hallway?" Jolene asked.

"Sure. I can use the space under the staircase for the one downstairs. That would be the easiest way to do it, though the shape might be a bit odd. It will also save you some money," Lee told her.

"Thanks Lee, I appreciate that. How soon can you get started? There will be other projects that I'll need help with, too. But for now, I'll be happy with closets," Jolene smiled at Lee.

"Well, now that I have the measurements, I can pick up what I need this afternoon. Is tomorrow too soon?"

"Tomorrow would be great! Thank you so much!" Jolene could barely contain her excitement.

"In that case, I'll be here tomorrow morning at eight," Lee smiled.

"Great! I'll see you then," she beamed.

Jolene was up early the next morning. For the first time in months she realized, she was happy. The stress of the last year, along with the move, had taken a toll on her. Now, with Lee coming out to work on the house, she finally felt as though things were moving in a positive direction. There was something about fixing up the house that made her happy. Or was it having Lee around that explained her good mood? After all, he was cute, with a sunny disposition. After constantly walking on eggshells around Garvin, it was nice to be around someone she could be herself with. "For God's sake, Jolene, he's a contractor. Not a boyfriend. You don't even know anything about the guy," she scolded herself. "Get a grip. Stop acting like a damn schoolgirl."

Promptly at eight, Jolene heard Lee's truck as he parked behind the house.

"Good morning!" Jolene called out.

"Morning ma'am," Lee replied.

"Please, call me Jolene," she said. "Ma'am makes me feel old."

"Sorry ma'am. I mean, Jolene," Lee blushed as they both laughed.

"Can I make you anything? Coffee?" Jolene asked, as Lee carried in various tools.

"No thanks. I'm good," he replied. "I figure I'll start with the ones upstairs, if that is ok with you."

"Sure, that's fine. Can I help you carry anything?"

"If you don't mind," Lee said as he handed Jolene a tool box. Their hands touched, and Jolene felt a shiver go through her. She blushed, then followed Lee up the stairs.

Lee frowned as he cleared the plaster from the hole in the wall. It was the first time all day that Jolene had seen him not smiling.

"What is it?" she asked.

"Well, it's just something I was worried about. This house has balloon framing."

"What is balloon framing? Is that bad?" asked Jolene nervously.

"It's how these old houses were built. See here. If you look up, you can see all the way up to the attic. The problem is, if there is a fire, it acts like a chimney. All the air gets sucked up the wall, bringing the flames with it. Nowadays, houses have fire breaks in the walls to slow things down." Lee noticed the worried look on Jolene's face. "Don't worry, I'll add some firebreaks as we go along. As a fireman, I couldn't leave it this way."

"You're a fireman, too?" asked Jolene. *Be still my heart.*

"Yes. I'm also an EMT. It's all volunteer out here. Believe me, we need all the help we can get. Any chance of talking you into joining us?" Lee smiled.

"Actually, I used to be an EMT back in New York. I'll certainly think about it," Jolene smiled back.

"Good, we'd love to have you." Lee turned back to the missing wall. He cleared the rest of the old plaster wall out of the way, then stopped. "What's this?" he asked, reaching into the open space. A few seconds later, he pulled something out, handing it to Jolene.

"It's a necklace," she said with surprise. "What is a necklace doing in a wall?"

"With the balloon framing, it's possible it fell from the attic. Maybe got hung on a nail," Lee said thoughtfully. "You never know what you'll find in these old houses. I've even heard stories of people finding money hidden behind walls, especially in houses owned by older people. They tend to not trust banks. They'll hide money all over the place." Lee shook his head, smiling.

"Really? I wonder what else we'll find in this place," Jolene said, studying the necklace. It was a cameo of a rose, carved in bloodstone. It was set against a gold background, with ornate gold filigree around it, on a gold chain. "This is beautiful."

"It looks old. I don't know that I've ever seen a black rose," Lee commented.

Jolene studied the necklace. "It's bloodstone. See how it's black, with red running through it?" She held the necklace up. Lee studied the stone.

"It's beautiful. But also, a bit spooky," he said.

"Yes. It is. I've seen rings made from bloodstone, but never anything carved like this. It really is unique." She rubbed her thumb over the rose, then looked at the wall. "If these walls could talk, I bet they would have some stories to tell."

"I'm sure they would. As old as this house is, there is a lot of history here," Lee agreed. He reached inside the wall again. This time he pulled out a snake skin, showing it to Jolene. "Here's something else you tend to find in these old houses. Most of these places have mice. The snakes come in looking for a free meal. You might want to set out some mouse traps. Or get a cat."

"Ugh," Jolene said, cringing at the sight of the snake skin. "Now I'll be up all night listening for snakes."

Lee laughed, "Welcome to the country."

The old house was quiet. Fog silently wrapped itself around the house, the farm light on the pole in the back yard was giving off an eerie glow in the darkness. Outside, a creature of the night hurriedly slunk past, trying not to attract the attention of any predators lurking in the brush.

In her bed, Jolene tossed and turned. She was finding the silence unnerving and was unable to sleep. She didn't know if it was the quietness of the night, or something else, but she felt uneasy. Staring at the ceiling, it was almost like she could feel the house breathing. A creaking caught her attention. It sounded as if someone was coming up the stairs. Heart racing, Jolene jumped out of bed, grabbing the flashlight. Apprehensively, she crept to the bedroom door, peeking out. The flashlight revealed only the empty hallway and staircase. Slowly, she made her way to the other bedroom, but once again, found nothing. With a nervous laugh, she returned to her bed and lay down. Just as she was beginning to doze off, she heard it. Scratching noises emanated from the wall behind her head. Jolene sat bolt upright in the bed. Something was in the wall.

Legs shaking, she got out of bed, turning on the light. The scratching noise stopped. She stared at the wall, not sure what she would see. She thought about the necklace. Maybe she should

have left it where she found it. Maybe if she hadn't removed it...
What if she disturbed something that didn't want to be disturbed?
There must have been a reason the necklace was hidden in the
wall to begin with. At the time, she thought it was an oversight.
But, what if it was some sort of warning? What if she had just
pissed off whatever was attached to it?

Jolene was beginning to think her idea of renovating the
old farmhouse might not have been such a good idea after all. As
a writer of paranormal murder mysteries, she thought the house
would be an inspiration. She now realized, she may have gotten
more than she bargained for. As she contemplated her next move,
a new noise caught her attention. A sliding sound in the ceiling
made her freeze in place. It almost sounded like...a snake. *Oh
Lord,* she thought, *Please, don't let there be snakes in the house.*
Almost as quickly, she thought of an alternative, something far
worse. Something she might find in one of her own novels. *Oh
Lord, let that be a snake.*

CHAPTER FOUR

Exhausted after her sleepless night, Jolene stared at the blank page on the computer screen and sighed. Last night, the sounds in the walls and ceiling had freaked her out enough that she had given up sleeping in the bedroom. Instead, she slept on the couch downstairs. Now, in the early morning light, she felt silly. It was an old house. Old houses made weird noises. When Lee came over to work on the closets, she would ask him to check the attic with her. She now felt sure there was probably mice. Okay, maybe even snakes in the house. With Lee's help, she was sure she could rid herself of whatever it was up there.

She got up, poured herself another cup of tea, and returned to the computer. She really needed to start the book. Marni couldn't hide the anxiety in her voice when Jolene told her she hadn't even begun the novel. With everything that had been going on the past few months, Jolene was not feeling up to writing. She also knew that she had a contract. Therefore, she had to come up with something. Soon.

She glanced at the necklace on the table. Picking it up, she fingered the rose, wondering about the woman that had owned the necklace. Who was she? What happened to her? How did the necklace end up in the wall? All sorts of scenarios filled her mind. Suddenly, she smiled. She had her book.

Rosemary stood up and stretched her back. She removed the broad-brimmed, straw hat from her head. Taking a handkerchief out of the pocket of her coveralls, she wiped her face. The sun was scorching, driving the temperatures well over eighty degrees. Rosemary glanced up at the sky. Not a cloud to be seen. They desperately needed rain. She surveyed her garden. The vegetables were holding up, but not for much longer if they didn't get rain soon. Sighing, she picked up the basket. She turned to head back to the house, stopping only to quickly add a few more tomatoes. The gardening took her longer than usual this morning. She knew she better get back to the house and get Bobby's lunch ready. Lord knows how mad he would be if he came in from working the fields and lunch wasn't ready. She didn't want to risk his anger. As she approached the house, Rosemary sighed. She knew it would only be slightly cooler inside. The windows were open. The fans were turned on. But, it was still a stifling Virginia summer day.

She climbed the porch steps to enter the mud room, allowing the screen door to slam closed behind her. After hanging her hat on a hook by the back door, she walked into the kitchen. Placing the basket next to the sink, Rosemary quickly sorted the vegetables she had picked. She could hear the sound of the tractor approaching. She knew Bobby was on his way. She hurriedly made a couple of sandwiches. She was setting the table when she heard the screen door bang close. Glancing at the door, she saw Bobby enter the kitchen.

"Damn, it's a hot one out there," Bobby drawled. He walked over to the refrigerator, opening the door.

"I just made some sweet tea," Rosemary told him.

"I don't want no sweet tea," Bobby snapped. "I want a beer."

Rosemary cringed as she watched him get a beer, guzzle it down, then take another beer out of the refrigerator. It was going to be one of those days. She opened her mouth to tell him maybe he should slow down, but then thought better of it. Instead, she set the food on the table in front of him, then sat down at the other end of the table.

"Did you get all the hay cut?" she asked.

"Yeah," he said through bites of his sandwich. "Though as dry as it's been, we ain't gonna get much this year. We're gonna have to sell some of the cows. We won't be able to feed all them this winter." Bobby finished his beer. "Get me another beer."

Rosemary hesitated, then took a beer out of the refrigerator. She handed it to Bobby without saying a word. Quietly, she sat down again, and picked at her food.

"What's with you?" Bobby glared at his wife. "You gonna eat that?"

"I'm just not hungry, I reckon," Rosemary replied.

"Well then, pass it over here. I ain't gonna sit here and let you waste food we can't afford," Bobby demanded. "A man's gotta eat, if he's gonna keep this place going."

"Here you go," Rosemary said softly as she passed her plate to Bobby. She absently fingered her necklace, as she watched him wolf down the food and finish the beer.

Bobby stared at Rosemary. "I should sell that damn necklace. That gold in it has to be worth something. Then we would have some money to buy feed."

"No!" Rosemary's eyes widened. "This is the only thing I have from my grandmother! I can't sell it! Please!" She blinked back tears. Bobby had been talking about selling the necklace for months. Her fear was that he would follow through with his threat. Rosemary never took the necklace off. He was going to have to take it off her by force, over her dead body. The necklace, a bloodstone rose cameo set on a gold background, was all she had left of her family and it meant the world to

her.

"Fine. You can keep it. For now. But, if things don't change here soon, it's going to be sold."

"Thank you," Rosemary said quietly. Bobby grunted a reply, then stood up, and walked to the door.

"The tractor needs some work. I'll be back in time for supper." Looking around he continued, "Be sure you get this place cleaned up before I get back. It's a mess."

"Yes Bobby," Rosemary replied dejectedly, watching him walk out the door.

Jolene sat back from her laptop. She reread what she had written. She could feel the creativity coursing through her. It was a brilliant idea to write a story around the house she had just bought. She didn't know anything about the history of the place. She debated actually researching the history for ideas. Ultimately, she decided to wait. Let the story come through first. If she ran out of ideas, then she would look into the house's history, see what turned up. Jolene knew a lot of writers used outlines for their books but found she couldn't write that way. She would get a germ of an idea, which morphed into a vague thought. If all went well, the thought turned into a story line. She wrote whatever entered her head. She had a number of small notebooks that she carried around with her. When something came to her, be it a storyline, character, or bit of dialog, she would write it down. Usually, those became stories, but not always. She didn't even write in order. This book was a classic example. She was starting somewhere in the middle of the story. The beginning would come later. She remembered how it used to bug Garvin. He would get pissed off when Jolene got out of bed in the middle of the night to write something down, before she forgot it. Or, if she stayed up all night writing because that was when her creativity kicked in. *Well, now he didn't have to deal with her writing anymore. I'm sure Astrid doesn't get up in the middle of the night,* she thought bitterly.

Astrid and Jolene met in college, soon becoming best friends. Both grew up with only brothers. They thought of each other as the sister they never had. Jolene was a bit in awe of Astrid, with her long, straight, blond hair, and huge, blue eyes. Astrid even did some modeling during school to make money. Despite her stunning looks, Astrid was wickedly funny. It was something they had in common. Jolene had to smile when she remembered some of their adventures in college. Man, they had fun. Then the smile vanished. The pain overcame her. Tears came to her eyes. When Jolene and Garvin started dating, Astrid became distant. She never liked Garvin. Jolene was the one that encouraged Astrid to take the job as Garvin's assistant. Astrid wasn't interested in Garvin. Or so she said.

After several years, Jolene began to suspect things had changed. She saw the way Garvin looked at Astrid. She heard the change in the tone of voice when he talked about her. Her relationship with Garvin soured, nothing she did was ever good enough. Nothing she said was interesting. Then came the day she caught them together, in her own bed. The pain of the betrayal flooded through her. Jolene sobbed out loud.

"Damn both of you!" she cried. She let the tears flow, then pulled herself together. "I will get over this. You won't break me." Wiping her tears, she took a deep breath, then let it out slowly. Looking outside, she noticed what a beautiful day it was. Deciding what she needed was some fresh air, Jolene went out the back door.

Outside in the fresh air, she surveyed the farm. She headed towards the horse barn, which was directly across the parking area. The barn had a center room that had originally been a corn crib, but was now a tack room, with a stall on either side. Inside, the room was covered in spider webs. Jolene found remnants of corn cobs, some rusty horse shoes and a couple of rusty bits. On the wall, next to an old scale, were two wooden stall signs, hand carved with the names Kaiser and Mindy. She briefly wondered about the horses. Who owned them, what kind were they? Were they riding horses, or work horses? Judging from the bits she found, she guessed riding horses.

Not finding anything else, she left the horse barn, and headed to the main barn, which was about thirty feet to the right.

Reaching the huge barn, she first walked around it. One end was a run-in shed, opening into the field. The shed attached to the rest of the barn, separated by a wide aisle. The other side was a huge, open space, where bales of old hay were stacked against the back wall. Walking along the side of the barn, she opened a door that led into what had been a milking barn. The floor was cement, except for a trough cut out that ran the length of the room. Huge sliding doors were on either end. Ten metal stanchions with head gates were in the middle of the room.

Jolene could picture the cows entering through one of the sliding doors, then walking into the stanchions. Once settled in, they would be fed while the farmer washed their udders. The water would run off into the trough, and out the other end of the barn.

Udders washed, the farmer would then milk the cows. After milking, the cows would exit out the other sliding door, back into the pasture.

Jolene knew these days, much of this was automated, but it wasn't so long ago that all this was done by hand. Standing in the barn, seeing the setup in person, gave her a whole new appreciation for the work involved to get milk.

Leaving the milking room, she continued to the end of the barn. Here, she found a covered area, open on the end. She assumed this was where farm equipment would be kept.

Looking back towards the house, she saw another small building. Walking up to it, she realized it was a chicken coop. She opened the door and peeked in. Weeds covered the interior, and huge holes in the ground were a clear sign that groundhogs had moved in. Jolene briefly fantasied about having chickens one day. It would be nice to come outside and collect fresh eggs. Maybe once she got settled in, she would get some chickens. Maybe even a horse, or two. She smiled. Feeling revitalized, she headed back to the house.

CHAPTER FIVE

Garvin paced the room, holding the phone to his ear. An angry scowl marred his otherwise good looks. His assistant, Astrid, watched nervously. She had never seen him so angry. For the first time since she started working for Garvin, she felt afraid.

"Don't tell me you don't know where she is! You're her damn publisher!" Garvin roared into the phone. "God damn it!"

Garvin stared at the phone in his hand. For a moment, Astrid thought he was going to throw it across the room.

"Damn bitch hung up on me! Who does she think she's dealing with?" he yelled, then glared at Astrid. "I'm going to find Jolene if it's the last thing I do. She thinks she can run out on me? No way! I'm going to find her and drag her ass back here."

Astrid watched in fascination as the anger slowly left his face. Not completely. She could still see it smoldering. It reminded her of a fire. Initially, it burned hot and bright the flames leaping, crackling and snapping. Then, after the energy burns off, it becomes smoldering coals- still glowing. Still able to reignite at a moment's notice. That was what she was seeing in Garvin. She would need to be careful around him. Astrid didn't want to get burned.

"Your VIP guests are here," she spoke softly.

"All right. Give me a few minutes. Be sure they get the best table." Garvin owned a very successful, high-end restaurant in New York City. Sometimes, he found himself amazed at it all. Sure, he worked hard. He practically lived at the restaurant that bore his name. It was a far cry from his first business, a small bar out on Long Island. Garvin had turned what had been a failing business into a success. Wanting something bigger, he sold the bar, buying another struggling restaurant in the city. Several years later, he had turned it around. Now, Garvins Restaurant was the place to eat in New York. He looked at the framed reviews and stories that lined the walls of his office. Pictures of Garvin with various celebrities; actors, musicians and athletes were interspersed among the framed reviews.

Garvin was smart, well educated, rich and successful. Yet, it wasn't enough for Jolene. The scowl returned when he thought of his ex. The fact it was actually his fault she left never entered his mind.

"Damn her," he growled. Gathering his emotions, he smoothed his hair, checked his clothes were presentable, then left his office to greet his guests.

Marni hung up her phone, shaking. Garvin had been especially crazy this time. Poor Jolene. If this was any indication of what she had been dealing with, no wonder she left. Marni had known Jolene for close to ten years, ever since Jolene sent Marni her first manuscript. Marni didn't know Garvin well, they had only interacted at social events. But, he seemed nice. He was good looking, athletic and funny. He and Jolene seemed like the perfect pair. Until it all went so very wrong. She needed to warn Jolene. Marni knew it was just a matter of time before Garvin tracked her down. Jolene needed to be prepared.

"He's just being a baby. He needs a bottle," Jolene said with more than a touch of sarcasm. "Like, a bottle of Jameson."

"Jolene. I'm serious. I have never heard him like this before. He's been pissed off, but this was scary. He sounded demented. I'm telling you, he is obsessed with getting you back. He WILL find you. Are you prepared to deal with him?"

Jolene heard the tone in Marni's voice. She was beyond rattled. Jolene could hear what sounded like hysteria building. Despite her bravado on the phone, she was scared. If Marni, who was tough as nails, and had survived so much in her own life sounded like this, it must be bad.

"Okay, Marni. I'll be on the lookout."

"I'm talking more than that, and you know it. You need a bodyguard, or a big dog, or even a gun. Or all three," Marni stated. "Do you have any of those?"

Jolene looked around the room. There was no bodyguard. There was no dog. However, there had once been a gun. She shuddered as a memory of the last time she handled it popped into her head.

"I'll be all right, Marni. I promise. I'll get a dog. I'll put an alarm system in the house. Please don't worry."

"I can't help but worry, not after what happened. You're not just one of my authors, you're my friend. I don't want anything to happen to you." Marni's voice cracked. "Please, please, please, be careful. Keep me posted. Let me know if there is anything I can do to help."

"I will," Jolene blinked back the tears in her eyes. "You're the best friend I could ask for, Marni. I promise I'll look into more security tomorrow."

"Okay. Take care of yourself. I'll talk to you later this week. Bye."

"Sounds good. Bye." Jolene quietly hung up the phone. She took a deep breath, then slowly let it out. Garvin did sound like he was becoming more unhinged. If he did find her, it could get ugly. She would need to secure the house, but how? It was over a hundred years old, with lots of windows. Even the doors had windows in them. Jolene loved all the light, and the feeling of being outside. Already, she had watched deer, foxes, and other woodland creatures cavorting outside. But, all the glass made it easy for someone to break in. Not to mention, she was in the middle of nowhere. No one would know if something happened to her. Deciding to make a cup of tea, Jolene walked into the kitchen. She stared out the window, pondering her situation. She would go into town first thing tomorrow and inquire about some sort of alarm system. Then, she would go to the shelter. She was going to get a dog. Maybe even two dogs. Big ones. If Garvin was on the way, maybe a whole kennel of dogs. Jolene smiled at the thought. "Calm down. Just one dog should do it. One nice, big, dog."

She felt him watching her as she walked down the line of cages. The noise was deafening. The barking of the dogs echoed off the cement walls of the shelter, making it almost impossible to think. He was in the last cage, sitting patiently. He was watching her, not making a sound, as if trying to decide if she was worthy of his time. Jolene stopped in front of the cage and waited. After several moments, he stood up, walked to the front of the cage and stared at her. He was huge. Jolene couldn't tell what breeds he was, but whatever they were, they were big. She glanced at the name on the door: Gunner. "Battle Strong," Jolene whispered. "I have a feeling you were meant for me. I just hope you don't have to live up to your name." She turned to the attendant.

"Can I take him outside in the pen, please?" she asked.

"Sure thing." The attendant opened the door, attached a leash to the dog's collar, then led him out. "Follow me." Together they walked outside to the fenced in area. Jolene took the leash, led the dog inside, closing the gate behind her. She noticed several chewed-up dog toys on the ground, as well as a couple of tennis balls. She led the dog over to the bench. Sitting down, she unclipped the leash.

"Do you want to play?" she asked him, tossing a tennis ball. The dog was off in a flash, catching the ball before it even had a chance to hit the ground, returning to Jolene.

"Wow. For a big guy, you sure move fast," she laughed, tossing the ball again. They played for a while, before he came over and sat down in front of her. Jolene petted him. He was short haired, dark brown with white on his paws. He was also solid muscle. His long legs and oily coat suggested some sort of hound dog, but the build was more working breed. Probably Pitt, since that is what everyone seemed to have these days. His dark, intelligent eyes stared into hers. It didn't matter what he was. He had stolen her heart.

Jolene slept fitfully, tossing and turning in her bed. Across the room, lying in his new dog bed, Gunner watched her. Suddenly, he turned his attention to the ceiling. The scratching sound was soft at first, but then grew louder. A low growl emanated from his throat. Slowly, he stood up, circling the floor beneath the sound. Finally, he barked. Loud.

Jolene sat up, startled awake by the bark. She noticed him staring at the ceiling. He whined, then barked again.

"What is it?" Jolene asked, as she cautiously got out of bed. Then she heard it, too. The scratching was louder. "What the fuck is that?" Nervously, she looked around for some kind of weapon. She spotted the guitar case. Grabbing it, she climbed onto the bed. Holding the guitar case straight up, she raised it and banged the ceiling with it a couple of times. The scratching stopped. Jolene waited a few minutes, but the noise didn't return. Shaking, she got off the bed, putting the guitar back. Gunner watched her expectantly. He glanced up at the ceiling once, but then turned back to Jolene. Whatever had been in the ceiling was gone.

"It was probably a mouse. Or a squirrel," Jolene said. Though this scratching sounded too loud for either. She resolved once again to check out the attic. Gunner walked over, licking her hand, slowly wagging his tail.

"Good boy. Now, I think it's time to go back to bed."

She lay in bed, staring at the ceiling. Sleep was impossible. Her mind was racing, her imagination in overdrive. It has to be vermin, she told herself. Just because the house is old and makes weird noises, doesn't mean it's haunted. Or does it? She thought about the necklace again. Maybe she should put it back. She recalled Pele's curse. Legend had it that anyone that removed lava rocks, or sand from Hawaii would anger the goddess Pele, bringing them bad luck until the rocks were returned. People actually mailed back the lava rocks that they had taken, in an effort to change their luck. Maybe she was dealing with her own version of Pele's curse. Of course, she had no idea who she could be dealing with. Jolene knew she would need to do some research on the house. She needed to know what she was up against.

CHAPTER SIX

Rosemary absently threw the scraps to the hogs, her mind a thousand miles away. Normally, she was cautious when dealing with them. The hogs were huge. She knew they would eat anything. Including her, if she wasn't careful. The boar was especially evil, she didn't like getting anywhere near him. She didn't trust him as far as she could throw him. Since he weighed over four hundred pounds, that wasn't far.

But today, she wasn't thinking about hogs. She was thinking about Bobby and her life. Rosemary had been a city girl, longing to live out in the country. She wanted to grow her own food; live off the land. When she met Bobby, she thought she found a kindred spirit. At first, things were wonderful. They spent what little money they had to buy a farm out in the country. Soon, they had cows, pigs and chickens. Rosemary planted a vegetable garden. She learned how to take care of the animals. Bobby planted hay for the livestock. He also did the repair work on the place. Together, they built fencing and took care of the upkeep on the barns. It was hard work, but Rosemary loved it.

It didn't take long however, before the realities of living on a farm sunk in. Bobby became more demanding, and surly with the pressure. If there was either too much rain, or not enough, it affected how much food they had for the animals. A lack of rain also contributed to concerns about water. Not just for Rosemary and Bobby, but also the animals. If the well ran dry, they would be in a lot of trouble. To make ends meet, Bobby worked as a mechanic, fixing cars and tractors. Rosemary did what she could to ease his load, but it wasn't enough. He started drinking. She soon found he was a nasty drunk. She learned to avoid him at all costs whenever he was drinking. This wasn't exactly the life she envisioned.

Rosemary picked up another bucket of scraps, throwing them to the hogs. As she turned, her foot slipped in the mud. Off balance, she staggered, then fell to the ground. She glanced up in time to see the boar headed her way. Rosemary scrambled in the mud, unable to regain her footing. She knew she only had seconds before the boar would be on her. Heart pounding, she rolled to one side, just as the boar reached her. She screamed as the boar's tusks slashed her arm. In horror, she watched him turn, preparing for another charge.

From out of nowhere, Rosemary saw a brown blur rush at the boar. She realized it was a large, brown dog. The dog leapt at the huge hog, biting it on the snout. The boar let out an ear-shattering squeal, then turned and ran. The dog stood his ground, barking. Rosemary managed to get back on her feet. Blood ran down her arm. She quickly made her way to the gate, scrambling out of the pig pen. She stood at the gate, shaking and crying. The dog also left the pen, standing near Rosemary. He looked up at her expectantly.

"I don't know where you came from, but you saved my life," Rosemary knelt next to the dog, giving him a hug. She studied him. He was built like a tank. Dark brown, with just a bit of white on his paws. He looked like he could handle anything that came his way. She looked down at her bloody arm and muddy clothes. "I better get cleaned up and get this arm bandaged, before Bobby comes back. He's gonna give me hell for what happened. Tell me I'm stupid or clumsy. Come on, I'll fix you something to eat, you look like you haven't eaten in a while."

Wiping mud off her as she walked, Rosemary headed for the house, the dog trotting along behind her.

The ringing of the phone interrupted Jolene's concentration. She considered not answering it. When the ringing continued, she gave up trying to write and answered the phone.

"Hello?" Jolene heard nothing but static. "Hello?" She thought she heard a woman's voice, barely audible over the static. "Hello? I can barely hear you, we have a terrible connection." The voice was still faint. "I'm sorry. I can't hear you."

"Help me." The voice was faint.

"Excuse me? Who is this?" Jolene asked, not sure she heard correctly.

"Help me. Please, help me."

Gunner, who had been sleeping at her feet, got up. He paced the room, whining, nose in the air as if tracking a scent.

"Who is this? I can barely hear you! Please, speak up! Hello? Hello?" Jolene shouted into the phone. Suddenly, the line was clear. There was no static, just silence.

Jolene hung up the phone, waiting, but the phone didn't ring. "That was creepy." She looked at the call log to check the number, thinking she would call back. PRIVATE NUMBER. "Well, so much for that theory," she said. She was unsettled by the call. Who could it have been, and did they need help? Should she call the cops? And tell them what? That she got what was probably a crank call? Jolene looked at Gunner, who had stopped pacing. He was now sitting, watching her.

"Yeah, that must be it. Someone is just messing with me," she said, trying to convince herself. Still, she was a bit uneasy. She touched the cameo necklace resting at the base of her throat. "Yeah, I can just see the local cops now. Crazy New Yorker freaking out about a crank call." She tried a smile at Gunner. Glancing at her watch, she realized it was well after one o'clock. She was starving.

"What do you say we get something to eat, then take a nice, long walk in the woods?" Gunner wagged his tail, prancing excitedly next to Jolene.

"I'll take that as a yes," she laughed. She felt overcome with emotion. She stopped, hugging the big dog, who licked her face. She laughed again. "Hey, and guess what? I put you in the book. What do you think about that?" She laughed again. It was then she realized, she was happy. For the first time, in a long while, she was actually happy. To hell with Garvin, who needs him? I have a dog that doesn't care who I am, or what I look like. Gunner doesn't care if I can make small talk at social events, or if I'm dressed appropriately for them. He doesn't care if know what wine to serve with a meal, or any of that crap. With Gunner, I can be myself. He doesn't care, he loves me, unconditionally. Jolene heard Lee upstairs, hammering and smiled. She also had a good looking young guy making her some closets. Yes indeed, things were looking up.

Jolene walked upstairs to check on Lee. She stood in the doorway, admiring the work he was doing. She was also admiring Lee. After a few moments, not wanting to be caught spying, she spoke.

"This is looking great!" she exclaimed. It was true. Lee had designed nice, huge, walk in closets in the bedroom. She would have plenty of room for storage. "I can't believe you were able to get this much room for closets."

"Thanks," Lee stopped what he was doing. "I've got the sheetrock pretty much done. Tomorrow, I'll start the trim work. After that, the doors get hung, then everything will be painted. Have you picked out a color yet?"

"Not exactly. I have a couple I like. It may come down to a coin toss," Jolene smiled. Lee smiled back. Her heart fluttered.

"Well, you just let me know. I'll go pick it up," Lee said.

"I will." On impulse, she added, "Gunner and I are going for a walk. Do you want to take a break and join us?" Her heart pounded in her chest. What was she doing?

"You know, that sounds like a good idea. It's too nice outside not to take advantage. Winter will be here before we know it. Thanks," Lee smiled, putting down the hammer.

"Great! Let's go," Jolene smiled back.

They walked along the trail that wound through the woods. Gunner ran ahead, stopping to sniff various spots, then lifting his leg to mark his territory. He was clearly enjoying himself. Lee and Jolene followed at a slower pace, walking next to each other. The trail followed alongside a creek. Jolene stopped to watch a small waterfall.

"I could sit here all day," she said. "It's so calming and peaceful."

"Yes, it is," agreed Lee. He looked around, taking in the scenery. "It is really nice back here."

"Were you born here?" asked Jolene.

"Yep. Lived here all my life. I grew up just down the road," answered Lee.

"You've lived in the same place pretty much your whole life?"

"Yes'm. Most folks around here, the families stay pretty

close. Typically, you move out of your folk's place, but don't go too far. When you have farms, it's a lot of work. The families stay close, so they can help each other out."

"Did you know the people who lived here before me?" Jolene studied Lee's face as she waited for his reply.

Lee hesitated before answering slowly, "Uh huh. I knew a couple of the families that lived here. Some better than others."

Jolene sensed Lee was holding back. "It seems as though this place has been sold several times recently. Do you know why no one seems to stay for very long?"

Lee glanced away before answering with a question of his own, "What did they tell you about this house, before you bought it?"

"Just that the previous family was anxious to sell. For some reason, I assumed it was either a divorce, or someone lost their job. Maybe they could no longer stay there. But, I've noticed since I moved here, no one wants to talk about this place. So, what's the deal?" Jolene stared at Lee, waiting for his response.

Lee sighed. "Okay. I don't know a whole lot. Mostly just the rumors I've heard. I didn't know the last family at all, they weren't here long enough. It was a husband and wife. I would see them at the store, or around town. It was mostly small talk. There was something about them that didn't seem right. Like, they were always tense. Jumpy. Then one day, the house was empty, and they were gone. It was like they moved out in the middle of the night. The next day, it was for sale."

"No one knows why they moved out?" asked Jolene.

"The rumors are, the house is haunted." Lee noticed the expression on Jolene's face. He continued hurriedly, "Of course, that is just a rumor. You know how folks always want ghosts and such. It makes for more interesting talk."

Jolene thought for several minutes. "What about the family before them? How long did they stay?"

"They only stayed a year," Lee said quietly.

"Same rumor?"

"Yes."

"What about before them?"

Lee hesitated again. "I don't remember much about anyone else. When I was a kid, the house was vacant for a long time. The story was there was a young couple that lived here. They say the wife ran off with someone else. Then the husband was killed in a farming accident. I don't know why no one moved in. I was so young, I didn't even think about it. It was just another abandoned house. I think that is probably what started the stories about it being haunted."

"Well. That's interesting. Do you believe any of it?"

"Not really. But you know how people are. If there is a rumor that it's haunted, and the people that live here believe it…"

"You don't have to worry about me," Jolene told him. "I believe in ghosts, I guess, but, I'm not going anywhere. If there are ghosts in my house, hopefully, they are friendly." She tried to make light of the conversation. "I guess we better get going." They continued on their walk. Jolene asked Lee about growing up on a farm. She listened while he talked about his life. It was such a different experience than she had growing up in New York. Before they knew it, they were back at the house.

"That was nice," she said.

"I hope I didn't bore you with my life history," said Lee.

"Not at all. I enjoyed it. Thanks for walking with me," Jolene smiled.

"My pleasure. I guess I better get back to your closets," Lee smiled back. Jolene smiled, watching him walk upstairs. Once he was back to work on the closets, she thought about their earlier conversation. For all her bravado, the news that her house was probably haunted was unsettling. She thought about the necklace that she was wearing, the noises in the walls, the phone call. Could she really explain all of it away that easily? What if there was something more going on? Two families she knew of left in a hurry. Not for the first time, Jolene questioned her decision to buy the house. Then, taking a deep breath, she steeled herself for the challenge. "I'm not running anymore," she said out loud. "You hear me? I'm...not...running!"

CHAPTER SEVEN

Garvin sat at the end of the bar. Nursing a drink, he surveyed the restaurant. His keen eye missed nothing. Years in the restaurant business taught him what to watch for. Bartenders watering down drinks, even stealing liquor. Busboys stealing tips from the wait staff. The wait staff not paying enough attention to their tables, mixing up orders, or even letting food get cold while they went outside to smoke. Or get high. Garvin wouldn't tolerate any of it. When he caught employees in the act, they were fired immediately. It was his name and reputation on the line. He was not about to let a bunch of assholes ruin it. While friendly to the customers, smiling and joking with them, his staff saw a different side. They understood the look when he spotted something that displeased him. That was all it took. Just a look. New staff that hadn't been on the receiving end of "the look", were oblivious. It didn't take long for them to be on the lookout for it, if they wanted to keep their jobs. The rare fool who tried to argue with Garvin, despite warnings from other staff, soon found themselves on the receiving end of a tirade that left them shaking.

The bartender refreshed Garvin's drink. Garvin watched the bartender for a moment, pleased at the way she tended to the customers. The rest of the staff appeared to be on their toes. Garvin wasn't stupid. He knew things were different when he wasn't there, watching. Therefore, he made a point of showing up at odd hours. He didn't want his employees to know when he would be there. He was always there at some point, every day. It was what drove Jolene crazy. Garvin remembered how Jolene would complain about his crazy hours. She was forever after him to take some time off, do something other than the restaurant. She didn't understand the pressure on him. Restaurants were a notoriously difficult business, many closed after only a year. Garvin was determined his would be different. He knew it was only because of the hours he put in that Garvins Restaurant was such a success. He tried to explain to Jolene, but quickly lost patience. Now Astrid, on the other hand…

Garvin's thoughts strayed to Astrid, and he found himself getting aroused. He smiled. Astrid was hot, no doubt about it. She was willing to do anything, at any time. She also understood the business. Garvin knew Astrid only went after him because he was in charge. He had what she wanted: money and status. He knew if his situation changed, she would drop him like a hot potato. Loyalty was not one of her strong points. Poor Jolene found that out the hard way. All those years thinking Astrid was her friend. Meanwhile, Astrid was just biding her time, waiting for the right opportunity to strike. Astrid was cunning, which didn't endear her to many women. Most didn't trust her, and rightfully so. Jolene was Astrid's only woman friend. Garvin knew Astrid was jealous of Jolene. Everyone loved Jolene. She was bright, funny and caring. Jolene would help anyone. She was also a successful writer. Astrid couldn't stand it when people came up to Jolene, talking to her about her books. So, Astrid went after the only thing Jolene cared about: Garvin. He had to admit Astrid didn't have to try very hard to get him. He should have known, however, that she would not let their affair stay a secret. Astrid needed to show Jolene that she was superior. That she could take any man she wanted. While Jolene saw Astrid as a friend, Astrid saw Jolene as a rival. One that needed to crushed. Astrid was incredibly competitive. For her, it was all about winning.

Garvin didn't love Astrid, any more than Astrid loved him. They might say the words in a moment of passion, but it was a lie. He hated to admit it, but he still loved Jolene. Astrid served a purpose. He knew they looked good together at social events, but he also found people seemed put off by her. While stunning, she lacked the warmth of Jolene. People were drawn to Jolene. Garvin needed her back in his life. It wasn't the same without her. He would find her and bring her back. No one ran out on him. Astrid wasn't the only one that didn't like to lose. He smiled again. Jolene didn't know what was heading her way. He was on the hunt. Let the games begin.

Astrid watched Garvin as he sat at the bar. He really was handsome, especially when he smiled. She had to admit, she felt a sense of pride in her success at stealing him from Jolene. Except, it really had been too easy. She scowled when she remembered his obsession with getting Jolene back. Astrid hadn't counted on that. She was aware if Jolene returned, the affair would cool down, if not actually be over. Astrid was not giving up her new-found status that easily. She glanced around the restaurant. A couple of the staff caught her eye, then glanced away quickly. Astrid knew the staff resented her. They all loved Jolene, of course, and resented Astrid for what she had done. *To hell with them,* she thought. *Who cares what they think? They are just jealous.* She had to come up with a plan. One that would prevent Jolene from returning. Several fantasies came to mind. What if… She smiled. Garvin's temper was well known, as was what had happened with the gun. What if Jolene ended up dead? The trick was Garvin had to survive. If he was killed, then she was back to square one. Astrid contemplated the situation. This might just work. She needed to think about it some more. Make sure she had a plan that could not fail. It could be done. She would have Garvin to herself. Jolene would be out of her life once and for all.

CHAPTER EIGHT

"What did I tell you?!" yelled Bobby. "You could have been killed! And then what? Huh? How could you be so damn stupid?!" Rosemary cringed as Bobby threw his empty beer bottle at the wall.

"I said I was sorry!" cried Rosemary. "It was an accident! If that dog hadn't shown up and scared the pigs away..." Rosemary broke down in sobs.

"I've told you a hundred times to be careful! Do I have to do everything around here? Do I?! Don't I do enough? All you have to do is feed the damn animals! And you can't even do that right!" Bobby grabbed her by the arm, shaking her.

"Bobby, stop! Please! You're hurting me!" Tears streamed down her face, as she begged him to stop. Bobby threw her across the room, where she landed in a heap, cowering.

"You are useless!" he spat. "Hear me?! Useless!" Storming to the refrigerator, he grabbed a beer, deftly popping the top off. He surveyed the room. "This place is filthy. It better be cleaned up by the time I get back. You hear me?!"

"Yes Bobby," sobbed Rosemary. With a final glare at Rosemary, Bobby guzzled the beer, throwing it against the wall next to the first beer. The bottle shattered, and Bobby laughed when Rosemary flinched at *the sound. Without another word, he got another beer, and left the house.*

Rosemary stayed on the floor, crying for several minutes. How she hated him when he was like this. Why couldn't things be the way there were when they first got married? When they were in love. Now, Rosemary realized, Bobby didn't love her. She was just there to cook, clean, and help with the farm. She was the help, nothing more. Except when he wanted sex, she thought bitterly. Then she was expected to perform her wifely duties, which consisted of her lying there while Bobby pumped away. When he was done, he would roll over and go to sleep, completely ignoring her. No kissing, no kind words, nothing. She would feel degraded and used. It was in those moments that Rosemary fantasized about Bobby being killed in a farming accident. The way his drinking was escalating, there was a good chance of that. She used to wish she was the one that would die, at times even thinking about shooting herself. She knew how to use the gun. Bobby insisted on teaching her. He said living out in the country, you needed to protect yourself from bears, or mountain lions. Sometimes she dreamed of running away, but to where? Plus, despite everything, she loved the farm. Getting up, she washed her face at the sink, then sighed. She needed to clean up before Bobby returned. She shuddered to think what would happen if she didn't.

The dog was lying under the trees, in the shade, when Bobby left. He watched as Bobby got in the truck, heading down the driveway. He turned his head towards the house, waiting. When nothing happened, he sighed, lowered his head onto his front paws, and watched.

"Did you get a dog?" Marni asked.

"Actually, I did," smiled Jolene. "I went to the local shelter, and there he was. It's almost like he was waiting on me to show up. I've named him Gunner."

"That's great! Now, I won't worry about your safety quite

as much. He is a big dog, right?"

"Of course! He's huge. I don't know what breeds he is, but he is quite handsome."

"Good. If Garvin shows up, now you have some protection."

"Marni, be serious. Garvin isn't going to show up. He has Astrid. Why on earth would he chase after me? He doesn't love me anymore," Jolene tried to be upbeat, but couldn't keep the sadness out of her voice. Marni heard the sadness and was concerned for her friend.

"How are you, really?" she asked sympathetically.

"I'm okay. Gunner is helping. It's not so lonely with him around," Jolene answered.

"How is the house? Have you started working on it yet?" Marni asked in an attempt to veer the conversation in a more positive route.

"Oh yeah!" Jolene perked up. "It is old, that's a fact. It's also in serious need of TLC. But, there is something almost familiar about it. I am really starting to feel like this is my home. Oh, I found a wonderful contractor, who is building me some closets to start with. Once that is done, we'll talk about a new kitchen," Jolene said brightly.

Marni noticed the change in tone, "By any chance, is this contractor young and handsome? And single?"

"It was that obvious?" laughed Jolene.

"Yes, to all three. Plus, he's a nice guy. But, before you say anything else, I'm not looking for romance right now, so don't get your hopes up. He's just a friend."

"Whatever. I've heard that before, too," laughed Marni. "I'm just glad you a have a friend down there." Marni paused, then continued, "Have you started the book yet?"

"Yes, I have. Let me tell you what happened. Lee, the young and handsome contractor, found an old necklace in the wall when he was working on the closets. It's an old cameo necklace. We figure it's probably close to a hundred years old. Anyway, it got me thinking about writing a book around who may have owned the necklace. You know, have it take place on the farm."

"What a cool idea," said Marni. "Do you have any idea who it belonged to? Or any history of the house?"

"Not really. Lee told me he grew up around here, but most of the families that lived here didn't stay long. Rumor is, the place is haunted. And, honestly, I've had a couple of experiences that make me wonder if the rumors are true."

"Only you Jolene," laughed Marni. "That is just perfect. Sounds like you'll have plenty of inspiration."

"No kidding."

"But, all joking aside, please be careful. I know you don't think Garvin will come after you, but I'm not so sure. He doesn't like to lose. If he thinks you leaving makes him look bad, he won't be happy about it at all."

"Don't worry about me, Marni. I've got Gunner. I'll be okay. No one knows where I am. It's a big country. Garvin will have to spend a fortune to find me. And, we all know how cheap he is. He'll fuss for a while, then go on his way with Astrid." Jolene wished she felt as confident as she sounded. As much as she didn't want to admit it, there was that nagging feeling that Marni was right. Garvin did hate to lose or look the fool. Who would want to leave him? Except, he did humiliate her by having an affair with her so-called best friend. She looked over at Gunner.

"You better live up to your name, dude. I have a feeling we're going to be getting some unwanted company."

Jolene took a shower and let the hot water pound her neck and shoulders, washing away her uneasiness following the phone call from Marni. She tried to put Garvin and Astrid out of her mind. She didn't want to think about them. If only Marni would let it drop. The whole point of leaving and moving to the country was just that. Leave it all behind. Start over. She wanted to think about her new life, the house, Lee…and the book. She felt good about the story she was writing. It was cathartic. She could use her feelings about Garvin and how he treated her, in the book. It was one of the advantages of being a writer. It was therapy, only a lot cheaper. In her book, she could kill off a character. If that character just happened to resemble an ex-boyfriend… It's all fiction, after all. Jolene smiled. *Poor Bobby*, she thought, *he was in for a rough time.*

She was snapped out of her reverie by a sound coming from the showerhead. The water hissed, sputtered, then resumed its flow, only to sputter again. It would shoot out forcibly, then stop, only to shoot out again, accompanied by a clanking sound in the pipes.

"What the hell?? Ow!!" Jolene quickly turned the water off, listening. The hissing and clanking faded away. Soon the only sound was her ragged breathing, along with the water dripping off her shivering body. Wrapping a towel around her, Jolene stepped out of the shower. She paused a moment, then turned on the water. After a few hiccups, the water returned to a normal flow. She turned it off.

"Probably just air in the pipes," she said. Picking up another towel, she bent over to rub her hair dry. Standing up, she turned to face the mirror. Her blood ran cold. In the steam on the shower door was written, *HELP ME.* Jolene stared as the steam cleared. All that was left was her reflection in the mirror. She saw how pale her skin was, her eyes wide. She could feel her heart pounding in her chest. She spun around. Tentatively, she reached out and touched the door, feeling the cool glass beneath her fingers. She couldn't possibly have seen what she thought she saw. It had to be her imagination, stirred up by the shower acting up. Even though she added paranormal events in her books, Jolene wasn't sure how much she believed in it. She always felt there was a logical explanation for everything. Almost everything. Now, staring at the door, she was having a hard time coming up with one. Maybe she had imagined it after all. She remembered the phone calls. The woman's voice asking for help. Did she tell Lee about that? Maybe he had written something on the door as a prank. That must be it. Except… she was fairly certain she hadn't told Lee about the calls. That left her overactive imagination. After all, her house was supposed to be haunted. It must be the power of suggestion. Alone in the house, in the dark, every little creak, groan, clanging, suddenly seemed paranormal. Jolene laughed nervously. Hard as she tried, she couldn't quite rid herself of the unease that had settled on her.

Wrapping her robe around her, she left the bathroom and hurried upstairs to the bedroom to get dressed. Gunner followed her, then jumped up on the bed. He circled a couple of times, before plopping himself down on the covers.

"Just make yourself comfortable," Jolene said. "Don't let me disturb you." She sat on the bed next to her dog. Absently, she stroked his head. She could feel the tension leave her body. She was being silly, she decided. It was just the stress she had been dealing with. Obviously, her imagination was running overtime. Jolene lay back on the bed and closed her eyes. Soon, she was fast asleep.

CHAPTER NINE

Lee sat in the truck, watching Jolene in the yard playing with Gunner. He smiled. She looked so free and happy, something he hadn't seen very much these past few days. She had been tense and distracted. Lee assumed it had to do with the book, or maybe her ex-boyfriend in New York. He wanted to ask her about it, but always chickened out. Lee knew he was falling for Jolene, but had no idea how she felt about him. She was friendly towards him and seemed to like him. But, for all he knew, she was that way with everyone. It didn't mean she saw him as anything other than just a friend. Or, a contractor. He drummed his fingers on the steering wheel. Maybe he should just ask her out. What was the worst that could happen? If she wasn't interested, she would say no. Then he'd know where he stood. But, maybe she would say yes. He was just going to have to go for it.

Climbing out of the truck, he put on his tool belt. Grabbing a few more items, he headed to the house. Jolene stopped playing with Gunner when she spotted Lee. Her smile lit up her face.

"Hey. I really love the way the upstairs closets came out. You did a great job!" she enthused. "Are you ready to start the one under the stairs?"

"Yes ma'am", Lee smiled back. "I'm glad you like them. I'm going to take the measurements first. Then I'll figure out how I want to build this one. It shouldn't be too hard."

The two of them walked into the house. They proceeded to the stairs, where they stopped. Lee stared at the staircase, walking back and forth as he pondered what he would do.

"The door won't be very wide, but I can put it here," he said, demonstrating with his hand how tall and narrow the door would be. "Inside, the closet will be a bit deeper. You'll have all the space under the stairs. Of course, the ceiling will get lower on the right side because of the stairs. Still, it should be good for storage."

"That's fine," Jolene said. "I'll take whatever space you can come up with. In fact, I've got a few more ideas for this place, if you have time." She looked up at Lee, hopefully.

"Sure thing. What kind of ideas did you have in mind?"

"A bunch!" Jolene laughed. "This place needs an overhaul."

"Well, you just let me know what you'd like done, and I'll get you an estimate. Then we can work out the details," Lee smiled.

"Don't worry. I'll have something soon," Jolene smiled back. "Actually, there is something that needs attention sooner. I've been hearing scratching noises in the walls and ceiling. I'm thinking it's probably mice, or squirrels. Do you think you can help me check out the attic? You know, make sure nothing is living up there?"

"Sure thing. I'd almost bet you have varmints up there. Most of these old places do. Don't worry, I'll take care of it. You don't want anything in here chewing the wires. We see a fair amount of house fires from that," Lee looked solemn for a moment. Then he smiled. "I didn't mean to worry you. It will be fine. I can take a look around once I'm done here. Then tomorrow, I'll fix whatever needs to be done. If that's okay with you."

"That would be great! I hate to admit it, but it was starting to freak me out a bit. I did think about the wires getting chewed. Fires scare me, so I'll be glad when I'm vermin free."

"Alrighty then," he laughed. Putting on protective glasses, he picked up the saw. "I better get started. I have vermin to banish from the castle."

Jolene was excited. The house would get fixed up. As an added bonus, Lee would be hanging out longer than she originally planned. She really needed to find out if he had a girlfriend. But then again, she had no idea if he thought of her as anything more than a client. Speaking of work, she needed to do some herself. Now that Marni knew she was writing, it wouldn't be long before she started pressuring her for the book to be done.

Jolene watched the cursor on her laptop blink. The blank page mocked her. Downstairs, she could hear Lee rummaging around below the stairs. She needed some inspiration. Her mind wandered to Lee. She thought about how good his butt looked in his coveralls. She thought about Garvin, and how he was always expensively dressed. Garvin wouldn't be caught dead in coveralls. Jolene smiled wryly, trying to imagine Garvin in coveralls, or doing manual labor. Not likely. Not as long as he could write a check to get it done. Garvin worked hard to build his restaurant, but doing contractor work wasn't his thing. Feeling a pang of uneasiness, she shifted her thoughts back to Lee. He was such a quiet, gentle soul. At least that's how he appeared to her. What did she really know about him, anyway? For all she knew, he could be a serial killer. Hiding behind those soft eyes, and

Southern drawl. Ok, she needed to stop. But then again, she was looking for inspiration. What about a good ole boy, who just happens to be a killer? With a smile, she started typing.

Absorbed in her work, Jolene jumped when Lee spoke.

"Sorry ma'am. I didn't mean to startle you," he said apologetically.

"It's okay. I was just writing a spooky scene. I guess I was a bit involved in the whole thing. And stop calling me ma'am!" Jolene laughed.

"Yes, ma'am," Lee blushed. "I was going to ask if you wanted to come up in the attic with me. I'm fixing to go up and see what you got."

"Sure. Do I need to bring a bat, or something to protect us?"

"Nah., I think we'll be okay," Lee laughed. "Ready?"

"Yep. Let's do this," Jolene replied. "You're sure I don't need to bring anything with me?"

"I'm sure," Lee answered as they made their way up the stairs. Stopping in the hallway, he reached up to what appeared to be a door, pulling it down. The door revealed itself to be a retractable ladder. Lee climbed the ladder slowly. Stopping at the top to look around the attic, he continued into the room. Jolene followed closely, also pausing at the top to glance around. Finally, they were both standing in the attic.

"Some of this flooring doesn't look too good. It looks like they just laid down loose boards, so this area could be used for storage," Lee advised. "Watch where you walk. You don't want to fall through the floor."

Jolene carefully followed Lee as they began their exploration of the attic. Lee examined all the walls, looking for holes where squirrels may have chewed their way in. Finally, he stopped. He pointed to the west gable end of the house, where the afternoon light was shining through.

"See that?" he asked Jolene. "See that hole? I'd say you have squirrels. I can put some rat wire on that, then cover it with plywood. That should keep them out. I'll also set up a trap, just in case they're hiding out in here when I close off the hole. Of course, that doesn't mean they won't chew back in somewhere else, but we can check out the trees around the house. Maybe trim them back a bit. Make it less inviting."

"Thank you so much, Lee, you're a lifesaver!" Jolene felt her unease about the noises fading. Her house wasn't haunted after all. It was just squirrels. Well, except for the writing on the shower door, the phone calls… There had to be a logical explanation for those, too.

"Jolene, you there?" Lee asked. She realized he had been talking, but she hadn't heard a word.

"Oh, I'm sorry. I was just thinking how nice it is that the scratching noises can be explained. And, that it's not paranormal," Jolene answered with obvious relief.

"I'm glad I could put your mind at ease," Lee smiled. "I'm pretty sure I even have the necessary parts to do this now. Let's go back downstairs. I'll check my truck." Turning back to the stairs, they cautiously made their way out of the attic. Lee went outside, where after rummaging around in his truck, he returned with the rat wire and plywood. Whistling, he went back to the attic. Jolene opted to pour a couple of glasses of sweet tea for them.

"Here you go," she said as she handed a glass to Lee when he returned.

"Thanks," he said, taking a huge swallow. "This is just what I needed. That attic got downright stuffy once that hole was patched. I checked around. I didn't see any squirrels. But, if you hear anything, let me know and I'll get a trap up there. I didn't have one with me today."

"Thanks again. I'm really grateful for all your help. How much do I owe you?" Jolene asked, reaching for her purse.

"Aw, don't worry about it. That was on the house. It didn't take no time to fix," Lee replied.

"Well, I really do appreciate it. I meant what I said. You have been a lifesaver. I had no idea what I was getting into buying this place. There is so much work that needs to be done!"

"Well, I'll do whatever I can to help. We'll get this place fixed up before you know it." Glancing at his watch, Lee continued. "I guess I better head on down the road. Thank you for the tea. I'll be here first thing tomorrow morning to work on the closet."

"Okay. I'll see you then." Jolene watched him walk to his truck. Setting his tools back in the toolbox in the bed of the pickup, Lee climbed in. With a wave, he drove down the driveway.

The house felt empty after he left. Suddenly, not wanting to be alone in the house, Jolene decided to take a walk before it got dark. She called to Gunner, and together they headed outside.

CHAPTER TEN

Rosemary hesitated, her hand hovering over the steak. She wanted to make something special for Bobby. Maybe if she made steak, he would treat her better. But, it was so expensive. She sighed, withdrawing her hand. There was no way they could afford it. Bobby would probably scream at her for spending the money. She stared longingly at the steak, then turned away and headed towards the chopped beef. Hamburger would have to suffice. She chose a package of the meat and tossed it in the shopping cart. After adding some bread and milk, she queued up in line to pay. The clerk was a teenage boy, with nice eyes and a friendly smile. He flirted with Rosemary, making her blush. She had to admit, even though she knew it was a harmless flirtation, it felt good to have a man pay attention like that.

Rosemary paid for the groceries, and with one last smile, left the store. She was still smiling as she loaded the groceries in the car. Feeling upbeat, she drove home. Her smile faded once she got home and saw Bobby's truck in the driveway. He was supposed to be helping one of the neighbors fix a tractor. She walked into the house, struggling with the door as she juggled the bags of groceries. Bobby was sitting at the table, drinking a beer. He watched her put the bags down on the counter, not bothering to help.

"Where you been? I'm hungry. Where is my lunch?!" Bobby slammed his fist on the table, making Rosemary flinch.

"I was at the store. Let me put these away. I'll make you something," Rosemary replied.

"You flirting with that boy?" Bobby glared at Rosemary.

"What are you talking about?" Rosemary turned to face Bobby.

"You know exactly what I'm talking about. I've seen the way you throw yourself at that boy. The one at the checkout. You're like a bitch in heat around him," Bobby snarled. Rosemary's heart beat faster, her hands shaking. She knew Bobby was drunk, and irrational. She had to tread carefully if she wanted to defuse the situation.

"Bobby, that's not true! You know you're the only one for me! You know I love you!" Rosemary's voice quavered. She prayed he would believe her. The truth was, she didn't love him anymore. At least not when he was drunk, which these days was most of the time. She wanted him to leave. She wanted to live her life in peace. Rosemary was tired of having to watch everything she said or did. She was constantly walking on eggshells, afraid of triggering Bobby's temper.

Bobby got up and walked over to Rosemary, then grabbed her jaw with his hand, forcing her to look at him. Rosemary tried not to show how much he was hurting her and stood very still. She could smell the beer on his breath.

"You think I'm stupid?! Do you?! I'll show you. You aren't going to make a fool out of me! I'll fix you. You just wait." Bobby shoved Rosemary back against the wall. "You... just... wait." With a final glare, he stumbled out of the kitchen. Rosemary slid down the wall until she was sitting down on the floor, unable to hold back the tears.

"I hate you. I hate you. I hate you," she cried softly.

Jolene sat back and glanced at the clock, surprised to see it was almost noon. Deciding to make something for lunch, she got up, glanced at Gunner sleeping on the couch, then headed to the kitchen. Returning with a tuna sandwich, she sat back down in front of the computer, ready to continue where she left off. Just as she was about to start typing again, she saw it. Below the last line she had written, was something that made her cold all over:

He's coming.

Jolene stared at the laptop. There was no one else in the house. She looked over at Gunner.

"Please tell me you can type," she said to the big dog. Gunner just snored. Jolene glanced around the room. How could this happen? She briefly wondered if she wrote it, without realizing it. But no, she was sure she didn't write that. If she didn't write it, how did it get there? The cursor blinked at the end of the sentence. With trepidation, she hit the backspace, watching as the two words disappeared. She jumped, letting out a short scream when the phone rang. Heart pounding, she picked it up.

"Hello?" she asked tremulously.

"Jolene? What's wrong?"

"Marni," Jolene sighed with relief. "Uh, nothing. It was just something I was writing. I think I freaked myself out, that's all."

"Well, that's a good thing, for a writer," laughed Marni. "If you are freaked out, just imagine what your readers will feel."

Jolene heard the smile in Marni's voice, but found she couldn't match it with her own. She was still shaken up.

"Yeah, I guess so," she replied, still staring at the laptop. *He's coming.* Who?

"Jolene! Are you listening to me?" Marni's voice brought Jolene back to the present.

"I'm sorry. What did you say?"

"I said, Garvin found out where you are. You need to be prepared."

He's coming. Jolene felt a flash of fear.

"How did he find out?" She tried not to panic.

"I'm sorry. I really am. It was that bitch Astrid. She sashayed her ass in here recently and cozied up to one of the new guys. He of course, didn't know your history. So, when she poured herself all over him like chocolate sauce on ice cream, he gave her your address. I'm so sorry Jolene. Needless to say, he no longer works here. But, Garvin now knows where you live." Marni's voice was strained. Jolene knew she was extremely upset. She knew Marni was fearful of Garvin, and what might happen.

"It's okay Marni," Jolene replied with resignation. "He would have found out anyway. It was just a matter of time." *He's coming.* Was that what the message meant? Was someone trying to warn her?

"You're too nice, Jolene. I really do feel horrible about all this. Please, please, please, be careful. Get the cops to come out and stand guard. Do whatever you need to do to protect yourself."

"He's not going to kill me, Marni. I'm sure if he shows up, it will be to yell and scream. He'll try to convince me to move back. If he was going to kill me, he would have done it by now." Jolene hoped that was true, anyway.

"Just promise me you'll be careful," Marni insisted.

"I promise. Don't forget, I have Gunner. Garvin is afraid of dogs. And, Gunner is huge. He won't want to come in. It won't be pleasant, but we'll be fine."

"I wish I had your confidence," Marni sighed.

Me too, thought Jolene. Not wanting to worry her friend any further, she forced a smile in her voice.

"It will be fine. I'm not the same, timid person I was back in New York. If Garvin shows up, he will be in for a big surprise. This little mouse will roar."

Jolene hurried home from the store, shifting the bag of groceries from her left arm to the right as she bounded up the stairs to the apartment door. Turning the key in the lock, she opened the door and entered, quickly shutting the door behind her. Locking the door, she continued to the kitchen, setting the bag on the counter. She hummed as she put away the groceries. Walking into the living room, she stopped. There, on the coffee table was a bottle of wine, and two wine glasses. One glass had lipstick on it. Jolene felt her blood run cold. She turned, heading upstairs to the bedroom. Reaching the top of the stairs, she stopped when she noticed the bedroom door was closed. A noise emanated from behind the closed door.

"Garvin?" Slowly, she approached. The noise stopped. Jolene hesitated, then opened the door. At first, her brain couldn't wrap around what she was seeing. Then, the shock hit her. In bed, in her bed, was Garvin. With Astrid. Her best friend. Jolene stared, stunned. The pain of the betrayal hit her like a ton of bricks.

"Jolene!" Garvin and Astrid scrambled to sit up, Astrid covering herself with a sheet.

"YOU SON OF A BITCH!" Jolene screamed. "HOW DARE YOU! AND YOU, YOU FUCKING BITCH! I TRUSTED YOU! I TRUSTED BOTH OF YOU!"

"Jolene, please, let me explain," pleaded Garvin as he stumbled out of bed, pulling on his pants.

"Fuck you! I don't want to hear anything you have to say! We are DONE! You hear me?!" Jolene turned to leave the room.

"Jolene, wait!" Garvin reached Jolene, grabbing her arm. Jolene spun around.

"Don't touch me! Don't you ever touch me again!" she screamed, eyes welling with tears. Garvin tried again to stop Jolene from leaving the room. Jolene turned and threw a punch at Garvin, connecting with his face.

"Damn it!" he roared. He grabbed Jolene, slamming her against the wall. "What the fuck?!" Jolene kicked Garvin in the knee, causing him to step back. Cursing, he reached for her again. Jolene ran to the dresser, yanking open the drawer. She pulled out a gun, pointing it at Garvin.

"Give that to me, before you hurt someone." He held out his hand, taking a step towards Jolene.

"Stop right there, or I swear, I'll shoot you." The gun wavered as Jolene's hands shook. Garvin stopped.

"Jolene. Please, give Garvin the gun," Astrid spoke up. Jolene turned, pointing the gun at Astrid.

"SHUT UP! I should shoot both of you! The only reason I haven't killed you both already is because I don't want to spend my life in prison. But, if you take one more step, I swear I will kill you, you bastard!" She pointed the gun back at Garvin.

"Jolene..." he began.

"I said SHUT UP!" Jolene suddenly pointed the gun at her own head. "Or is this what you want? HUH? Is it?! Both of you! Maybe if I just shoot myself, then you can be together without worrying about me! Is that what you want?!"

"NO! Jolene, stop! Please! Put the gun down!" Garvin begged. "We can work through this! Please!"

Jolene stared at Garvin, then Astrid. Finally, she lowered the gun.

"You're not worth it! Neither of you! Now, get the fuck away *from me!" she shouted. Garvin backed up a step. No one spoke. Tears streamed down her face. "I hate you. I hate both of you." Dropping the gun, Jolene turned and ran out of the room. Garvin started after her, but Astrid called out.*

"No, let her go!"

Garvin followed Jolene into the hallway, but stopped. He watched as she ran down the stairs, fumbled with the lock on the front door, then finally opened it and ran out into the night.

Jolene awoke, bathed in sweat, her face stained with tears. She thought she had banished that night from her memory. Obviously, not. The message on her laptop, along with the conversation with Marni, had triggered the dream. Wiping her face, she let the memories flood over her. After running out of the apartment, Jolene had fled to the only person she trusted: Marni. She remembered banging on Marni's door in the middle of the night, hysterical. Marni freaked out, of course. But, Marni soon had Jolene safely ensconced at her place. Jolene bared her soul to her, and Marni did her best to comfort her friend. Jolene ended up staying a week. Garvin called Jolene's phone constantly, begging her to come back. When she didn't answer the phone, he started calling Marni. Flowers for Jolene filled Marni's office. Jolene told Marni to throw them out. By the end of the week, she had decided to flee. Before she knew it, she and Marni were at the apartment while Garvin was at the restaurant, loading up her clothes and the few other items she wanted. Then, she was on her way south to start a new life in Virginia.

Things had been looking up. Until now. Now, Garvin knew where she was.

CHAPTER ELEVEN

It was the sound that woke her. The creak of the steps. Someone was coming up the stairs. Jolene was disoriented, the room dark. She glanced out the door, and saw a shadow moving down the hall. Jumping out of bed, she stood behind the door hiding. Heart racing, she thought about what was in the room. Was there anything she could grab as a weapon? There was only one way out. She would have to go in the hallway where she had seen the shadow. If someone was in the other room, it wouldn't take them long to find her.

Gunner hopped off the bed and stood next to her, tail wagging slowly. Cautiously, Jolene peeked out, but didn't see anything in the dark. She glanced again at Gunner. Surely, if there was someone in the house, he would bark, or even go after the person. Wouldn't he? Slowly, she left her hiding place behind the door. Creeping into the hallway, she hugged the wall like a roach. Shaking with fear, she made her way to the other bedroom. Gunner trotted past her, then stopped at the open door. His tail still wagging, he tilted his head, as if listening to something she couldn't hear. He whined, then sat. Jolene felt as if her knees would give out. She stopped at the door, reaching in to turn on the light. The room was empty. Leaning against the door frame, she surveyed the room. Gunner walked over to the closet where Lee had recovered the necklace and whined again. A bit unsteadily, Jolene approached the closet, then stood to the side as she opened the door. Tail wagging, Gunner stepped inside. Excitedly, he sniffed around for a minute before walking back into the room. Whatever he was interested in, clearly wasn't there anymore. Jolene started to turn away when something white caught her eye. On the floor of the closet, in the corner, was a piece of paper. She bent down and picked it up. It appeared to be one page of a letter. The writing was faint, barely legible. It was old, yellowed, and brittle. She pondered how this ended up in the closet. Why hadn't she or Lee seen it before now? Maybe because it was tucked in the back. She might not have noticed herself, if Gunner hadn't shown interest in the closet. Carefully, she lowered herself until she was sitting on the floor.

...I worry about you, my darling. I hate how sad and lonely you sound in your letters. Maybe you should come home, I miss you terribly. Please don't let him have the necklace, it means so very much to you. Hide it away, somewhere, keep it safe. Please remember how much I love you...

Jolene couldn't make out the rest of it. A chill went over her. She realized her arms were covered in goosebumps. This was eerily like what she had written in the book. *Of course it is*, she told herself. *After all, it was the necklace that inspired the book. It is just a coincidence.*

Standing back up, she carried the letter back to her bedroom where she gently set it down on the nightstand. She glanced at the clock, 2:30 in the morning. With a sigh, she crawled back under the covers. She barely resisted the temptation to pull them over her head and hide. Gunner jumped back on the bed. For once, Jolene didn't even care that he was hogging most of it. She was just glad to have another living being next to her. Despite Gunner's presence, she tossed and turned the remainder of the night, her brain refusing to shut down. Finally, just before sunrise, she fell asleep.

Lee sat on the porch swing, next to Jolene. Sandwiches and two glasses of iced tea rested on a small table in front of them. Lee reached over picking up the glasses, handing one to Jolene. They sat in comfortable silence for a moment, taking in the scenery. From the porch, they looked over a field of grass that ran down to a thicket. In the thicket, was a stream. On the other side of the thicket, a grassy field led up to a stand of pine trees. Jolene liked the hill. It blocked her view of the neighboring farmhouse. To her right, the property was wooded. They watched as a herd of deer bounded down the hill to the thicket, appearing on the other side of the stream. Alertly, they scanned the field. Not finding any predators, they settled down to graze the various grasses.

"It is so peaceful here," sighed Jolene.

"It must be quite a bit different from New York," offered Lee. Jolene smiled.

"How about, totally different?" she laughed. "I'm still adjusting. At first, I couldn't even sleep because it was so dark and quiet. New York City, as they say, never sleeps. There are lights blazing all night long. The noise from the traffic is unbelievable. Of course, when you live there, you get used to it. Planes fly overhead all day and night, trains, taxis, you name it. It is loud. Now that I've been away from it all, I can't believe I was ever able to sleep up there."

"Do you miss it?" asked Lee.

Jolene thought a moment before responding. "There are some things I miss. The beaches, for example. Also, the food. There are so many cultures. There is quite the assortment of restaurants. I don't miss the stress, all the people, the noise, and the garbage. It is so beautiful down here. I almost don't want people to discover it. Let them stay up there," she laughed.

Lee laughed, too. "That would suit most of the folks around here just fine. We have people move here from other places. Some are good folks, some are just…"

"Assholes?" Jolene smiled.

"Well, I wasn't going to put it quite that way, but yes. They move here and want to make all sorts of changes. Sometimes I feel like asking why they moved, if all they want is to have things like it was where they came from."

"I don't know. People can be ignorant. I guess there is something about wanting familiarity. I'm with you. Just stay where you are." They sipped their drinks and ate the sandwiches, the porch swing moving gently back and forth. "I can't believe how nice the weather is for November."

"We can have some downright hot days this time of year. It will get cold, don't worry. Enjoy it while it lasts. Do you mind if I ask you something?" Lee asked.

"Not at all. What is it?"

"It's about your books. You said you write murder mysteries. Where do you get your ideas?"

"Well, I get them from everywhere. It could be something I saw on TV, or maybe read in the paper. Or, conversations with people. I'll get a germ of an idea and go from there. Like the necklace. I started thinking about who owned it. What kind of life they may have had in this house. That, plus the stories you told me, just added to the plot. When I was little, my family traveled a lot. I would sit in airports, or even hotels and people watch. I'd imagine who they were, where they were going, or why there were here. I still do that, actually."

"The book you are working on, it's about this house?"

"In a matter of speaking, yes. Obviously, what I'm writing is fiction. I only know what you've told me about the people that used to live here. But, this house is proving to be rather inspirational. Especially with the strange experiences I've been having. I know some can be explained away. It's an old house, there are mice, that kind of thing. Even still, I'm finding it harder to come up with alternate, logical explanations for some of this stuff. Therefore, it goes in the book," Jolene smiled. "Which reminds me, can we check the attic again, please? I heard more noises again. I'm wondering if there might still be some small, furry, woodland creature lurking about up there."

"Sure, we can check. Those varmints can be quite persistent," Lee replied. "We can do that before I leave today."

"Thanks. I really appreciate it."

"It's no problem," Lee smiled back. Jolene stared into his eyes, feeling her pulse race. It was now or never.

"Now it's my turn," she said. "Do you mind if I ask you something personal?"

"Go ahead."

"Would you be interested in dinner with me tomorrow night?" Jolene held her breath, praying she wasn't going to look like a fool.

Lee smiled broadly, "I'd love to have dinner with you. What time?"

"How about six? I can make something here. My cooking skills are limited, but no one that has eaten my food has died. Yet. Not that I've heard, anyway," she smiled shyly.

Lee laughed. "I'll take my chances. I'm sure whatever you make will be delicious. Don't forget. I am an EMT, just in case."

"I feel safer already. Of course, if you get poisoned, you'll need to tell me how to save you, before you die."

"I will, don't you worry," Lee laughed again. Finishing the last of his tea, he stood up. "Now, I think I better get back to work. I don't want the boss lady getting mad at me goofing off."

Jolene also stood up. "That's right. Get back to work. Which is what I need to do, too." She gathered up the plates and glasses and followed Lee back inside the house.

"Well, I don't see any signs of varmints in here. The hole I fixed is still closed off. And I don't see new holes. Of course, mice and rats can squeeze through tiny cracks. So can snakes," Lee said as he surveyed the attic.

"Great," Jolene replied a bit sarcastically. "I forgot about snakes. Maybe that was the sound I heard."

Lee walked over to a corner of the attic, picking up the remains of a snake skin. "I think that is a good bet. Look at this. Snakes shed their skin. This one is huge. I'll be this snake is close to six feet."

Jolene cringed. "That's just what I need, a monster snake in the house."

"Look at the bright side. He's eating the mice," Lee laughed. Jolene shook her head.

"Wonderful. I'll be downstairs." Carefully, she made her way out of the attic, Lee following not far behind her. "Now that you've creeped me out about the attic, I have a question. I was looking at the closets you did. Would it be possible to extend the closet space further along the wall, and hide a body in it?"

Lee stumbled on the ladder. He stared open mouthed at Jolene, who broke out in laughter.

"Oh my God, you should see the look on your face," she laughed, wiping tears from her eyes. "Don't worry, it's research for the book. I'm not planning a murder."

"Are you sure?" Lee responded, nervously.

"Okay, pretty sure. There are a couple of people I wouldn't mind putting in a wall, or something. But seriously. I was trying to think of a plot line for the book. Usually, murderers tend to bury their victims in the basement, or crawlspace, or something. I want to do something a bit different. But, I don't want someone who knows more than I do about construction work write and tell me what I did isn't possible."

"Would they do that?" Lee asked, regaining his composure.

"Yes. I was talking to another author one day. She said she got a hateful email from someone, reaming her out because she had the wrong caliber ammunition in a gun. I must admit, I'm the same way. I'm super critical of books with horses, if something isn't correct. I don't know how many contractors read murder mysteries, but just in case, I want to be sure what I'm thinking of writing is possible."

Lee thought for several moments. "You could make space. An old house like this, sometimes you'll see where someone will add central air conditioning or something. The ductwork will be inside stacked closets. If the person isn't very big, it's possible you could put them in there. You're sure this is for the book?" Lee asked. Jolene smiled, touching his arm.

"Trust me. It's just a plot line. Unless, of course..." She saw the look on Lee's face and laughed again. "Come on Lee. I'm kidding. I can tell you haven't spent a lot of time around writers. You wouldn't believe the conversations we have. Not to mention our searches on the computer. You'd swear we were all serial killers."

Lee laughed, blushing. "Okay. But, if you start asking me to extend the closets, I'm out of here."

"My ex never wanted to discuss my books. Asking him questions like this freaked him out. I'm glad you're being a good sport," she smiled.

"Something tells me he might be a contender for some wall space," laughed Lee.

"No comment," Jolene smiled back, rolling her eyes. "Of

course, if you want to make a space to fit a six foot, one-hundred-and-sixty-pound man…"

"I'll pretend I didn't hear that. In case the cops question me," laughed Lee.

"Does this mean you'll bail me out?"

"Yes ma'am. You promised dinner, remember?"

"That I did. You make a good co-conspirator," she laughed again. "Now that you've answered my question, I better get back to the book."

"And I better get back to the closets. Normal sized ones," Lee said. Shaking his head, he headed back down the hall.

Bobby stepped back and surveyed his work. The space was small, but it would do. Nestled in the wall next to the fireplace, he had built a small closet. When facing the fireplace, the closet was to the left. It wasn't very deep, though would suffice for hanging up coats. The space extended to the right almost all the way to the fireplace. Like the closet, it was tight. Bobby, thin and wiry from doing the farm work, was able to fit in the narrow space. He blocked off the extra space with a sheet of plywood. No one would notice, unless they looked for it. He had plans for that space. But for now, it would be his secret. Rosemary was always complaining there wasn't enough space to store anything. She wanted a closet. Bobby resented having to build one. To him, that just meant they had too much stuff they couldn't afford. Stupid woman. Things had been strained between them. To get her off his back, he relented.

"This should keep her happy," he said. In order not to have a door open into the main room, Bobby installed a pocket door in the wall- not an easy task when dealing with lath and plaster walls. The whole project had been time consuming. Bobby thought of all the other things he should have been doing instead of this. Rosemary would get her space. He could go back to what he considered real work on the farm.

"Is it finished already?" Rosemary asked as she came up behind Bobby.

"Already? It only took me three damn days! You know how hard it is to redo lath and plaster?" snapped Bobby.

"I'm sorry. I just thought it would take longer. I'm impressed you finished it faster than I thought it could be done," Rosemary responded carefully. "It looks great! Thank you for doing it."

"Well, this doesn't mean go out and buy any more crap. If you have to put it in a closet, we don't need it. Now, I need to get back to work," he growled, stomping out of the room.

Rosemary fingered the necklace hanging gently at the base of her throat. Bobby was becoming more irrational every day. It was beginning to scare her. It was getting harder and harder to get him back to his normal self. She noticed the escalation in his drinking and tried to think of some way to stop it. Not able to come up with an immediate solution, she glanced out the window, and saw Bobby drive off in the truck. She quickly made her way up to the attic.

Walking across the room, she squatted down next to the far wall. Carefully running her fingers along the wall, she found a spot and pressed inward. A small, hidden door popped out, revealing a hidden compartment. Rosemary reached in, pulling out a handful of envelopes. She chose one. Carefully, she pulled out the letter. Her eyes welled with tears as she read. When she was finished, she put the letter back in the envelope. Then, she read the rest of the letters. When she was done, she gently put the envelopes back in the wall. Reaching up, she unhooked the necklace, placing it in the wall with the letters. She closed the hidden door, making sure it was not visible to all but the most critical eye. Wiping her eyes, she thought about the letters. If Bobby ever found them…

Rosemary shuddered to think of his reaction. She thought about how her life was turning out. She felt stuck with a husband that no *longer loved her but would never let her go. She was sure of that. Not that she could afford to leave. She had no money of her own. Everything was in Bobby's name. The only thing Rosemary had for herself was the necklace. There was no way she could ever sell it. A dark cloud settled over her. She wished again that Bobby was dead. In Rosemary's mind, that was fast becoming the only solution. She thought of the letters again. There was someone else that loved her. Someone that would take her back in a heartbeat. Someone she could start over with. So, why was she still here? Her only answer was, she loved the house. She didn't want to leave. No, she needed Bobby to leave. Or die. Sighing, she realized that would never happen. She was stuck. Filled with despair, she put her head in her hands and cried.*

Jolene sat back and stared at the laptop. She had started with a vague idea of a story. She was letting the story reveal itself. She had tried writing from an outline once. But, she found herself totally stifled and gave up. She may not be the speediest writer, but she got it done. She thought about the book. Already she found it wandering from her initial idea. She still knew what she wanted to happen but felt the book might take a roundabout way to get there. She also felt rather strongly that the house was influencing the story. Her books tended to be rather dark. After her last book, Jolene promised Marni the next one would be lighter, more of a "cozy mystery." She had a feeling Marni would not find anything cozy in this book. It was taking a dark turn. She glanced around the room. It was the house with its dark past. It was also all the bullshit with Garvin. Of course, the strange happenings going on weren't helping. There was no way in hell a book influenced by this house would turn out to be a cozy mystery. Especially with the ending she was planning. Oh well, Marni will just have to get over it.

Susan M. Viemeister

CHAPTER TWELVE

Jolene decided she needed to do some research on the house. She wanted to know more about the previous owners. She needed the history of the place. There were rumors. But, what was rumor and what was fact? She needed to find out. She decided to start her search with the real estate agent who sold her the house. Surely, he would know why the previous owners moved. Maybe he knew more of the background of the house. She found the number of the real estate agency, poured a glass of iced tea, and called the number.

"Bealtown Realty, Janice speaking," the voice answered.

"Hi. This is Jolene Turner. Can I speak to Dale, please?" Jolene asked. There was silence for a moment before Janice responded.

"I'm sorry, Miss Turner. Dale passed away last night," Janice answered somberly.

"What?! What happened? I didn't realize he was sick!" Jolene was shocked. Dale had been young and seemingly healthy.

"Well, actually, I'm afraid he committed suicide," Janice replied softly. Jolene could hear the pain and shock in the woman's voice.

"Oh my God! I'm so sorry! I just can't believe it. That is so sad," Jolene felt tears come to her eyes. "Thank you for letting me know."

"I'm sorry. Was there something you needed? Can I get someone else to help you?" Janice pulled herself back together.

"Um, no. That's okay. It wasn't anything important. Thank you for your time. And, again, I'm so sorry about Dale." Jolene hung up the phone and stared out the window. She hadn't known Dale long, or very well, but he always seemed happy and upbeat.

But then again, people are notorious for hiding their true feelings. It had obviously all been an act. Poor Dale. Feeling melancholy, her thoughts jumbled, Jolene walked over and sat in the chair by the window. Gunner entered the room, walked over and laid his head in her lap. Jolene absently stroked his ears.

"You always seem to know when I need you, don't you?" she smiled sadly down at him. Gunner just wagged his tail, his big eyes staring up at her. Jolene sighed. "Come on, let's go for a walk."

The phone rang as she returned to the house. Her thoughts still not quite focused, she answered.

"Hello?"

"Is this Jolene Turner?" a woman asked.

"Yes. Who is this?" Jolene responded cautiously.

"This is Janice, from Bealtown Realty. I'm sorry to bother you. I hope I'm not being an imposition. But, I looked up what house you purchased. I think I know why you called earlier. I may have some information for you. Can we meet this afternoon?" Jolene heard the tension in the other woman's voice.

"Sure. Do you want to come out here?" Jolene asked.

"No! I mean, I'd rather meet somewhere else. If that is okay with you," Janice stammered.

"Uh, sure. That's fine," Joline said slowly, a bit taken aback. She had the distinct feeling Janice wanted no part of her house. "Where would you like to meet?"

"There is a park just outside of town. Can we meet there in an hour?"

"Okay. I know where that is. I'll see you soon."

Despite the nice weather, the park was deserted when Jolene pulled in. There was only one other car in the lot. A lone woman sat on a bench nearby. She looked up when Jolene got out of the car. The woman had been crying. She was in her forties, bleached blond with a bad perm.

"Janice?"

"Yes, Jolene?"

"Yes." Jolene sat down next to Janice. "I'm really sorry if I upset you."

"Oh no, it's not you. It's just, I was really close to Dale. I still can't believe he's gone," she sobbed. Janice toyed with a crumpled tissue in her hand, then wiped her eyes. "I'm sorry."

"It's okay. Please, don't apologize," Jolene said soothingly. Janice wiped her eyes again. Taking a deep breath, she seemed to bring her emotions back under control.

"I guess I should get to the reason I asked to meet with you," she sniffed. "You called looking for information on your house, didn't you?"

"Yes. I did. There have been some strange things happening. I'm sure it's just my imagination…" she began before Janice interrupted.

"No. It is not your imagination. I probably shouldn't be telling you any of this. I could be fired. But after Dale… well, I just don't care anymore. You need to know what you've gotten into."

Jolene felt a chill go up her spine. She hoped she was prepared for whatever Janice told her.

"Go on. Please."

Janice took a deep breath, glanced around, then continued.

"Your house has a history. A bad one. There is something evil about that house. Anyone who has lived there or had anything to do with it ends up dead. People have died in accidents, been murdered, even committed suicide." Janice choked back a sob. "I warned Dale not to get involved with it. When it came up for sale, I told him about the stories. He just laughed and said they were only stories. I begged him, I told him no other real estate agency will touch it! He didn't believe me. I was so scared for him. He had no reason to kill himself! He was never the same after spending time in that house! And now he's dead, too!" Janice broke down in tears. "It's that damn house!"

Jolene didn't know what to say. Obviously, nothing she said would make Janice feel better. Did she really believe everything she was hearing? It was an old farm. Someone living in it years ago could have died from an accident. That made sense. Accidents happened all the time on farms. That didn't mean the place was evil, or even haunted.

"Janice..."

"Don't tell me I'm making this up! I'm telling you. I've lived here all my life! I KNOW this house! I knew people that lived in it. I saw what happened. No one will stay. They ALL end up leaving. The ones that don't move, they end up dead. You need to get out while you still can, before something happens to you!"

"Can't there be some other explanation? I mean, it's a farm. You said people died in accidents. That isn't unusual for a farm, especially working with farm equipment."

Janice stared at Jolene. "You aren't listening to me. I'm not talking about one accident. I'm saying that every family that has ever lived in that house suffered a tragedy. Every...family. Now, you tell me about another house where that happened. I've talked to some of the ones who saw...things. Dale spent time in that house, getting it ready to be sold. The previous owners didn't even take their belongings. Did he tell you that? They just up and

80

left in a hurry. Told him to do whatever he wanted with their belongings, they didn't care. They just wanted out. They moved out in the middle of the night. How many people do that? Dale had to clear out their stuff. That place got to him, I'm telling you!" Janice broke down in tears, bending over and covering her face with her hands. Her shoulders shook with her sobs. Jolene watched silently, not sure what to think. Suddenly, Janice sat back up.

"There was a young couple that lived there for several years. They tried to make a go of the farm but were always broke. Then one day, the wife up and leaves. Rumor was she ran off with another man. The husband sticks around, but then dies in an accident on the farm. The place sat empty for a number of years. Then another family bought it. They had kids, and also tried to farm the place. Then one day, one of the kids drowned in the pond. They moved away shortly after. People said it was because of the ghosts. The place would sit empty, someone else would move in. Next thing you know, the rumors started about it being haunted. People heard things in the walls or saw shadow people. Things would be misplaced or moved around when no one was home, that kind of thing. There was another family, the mother got real sick and died. It just goes on, and on. Now, no one even sticks around long at all. They up and move out after a year, sometimes even less. You said you had things happen. Now do you believe me?" Janice looked questioningly at Jolene.

"Yes...I've had things... happen," Jolene answered slowly. "But, I'm sure some of it was vermin in the attic. Some other things, I'm not so sure about."

"You need to get out while you still can," Janice implored.

"I'll be okay. Really. I promise," Jolene hesitated, not sure how Janice would respond to what she was about to say. Taking a breath, she forged on, "I've been thinking what I might do is, see if I can find someone familiar with the paranormal to check it out. Maybe like a psychic medium, or a paranormal investigator. Something like that. Perhaps if I can find someone that knows this stuff, they can tell me what is going on. Even how to get rid of it. Despite everything, I really do like that old house."

Janice didn't say anything, just stared at Jolene. *Great, now she thinks I'm a fruitcake,* thought Jolene. Finally, without a word, Janice grabbed her purse and rifled through it. A minute later, she produced a business card and wrote something on it. She handed it to Jolene.

"Here. Call this number. Tell him I gave it to you," she said, standing up. "Thank you for meeting with me. I really hope you change your mind. Once y'all start messing with the unknown, it can cause all sorts of havoc. You seem like a nice person. I would hate to see anything happen to you." Nodding at the card she continued, "Good luck." Jolene watched as Janice quickly walked away and got in her car. Gravel shot out from under the tires, as the car sped out of the parking lot. Sighing, Jolene glanced down at the card. Janice had scribbled a phone number and a name: *Professor Rupert Kozmo.*

CHAPTER THIRTEEN

"Where the hell is Bealtown? That is just so like Jolene to run off to some hole in the wall town, in the middle of nowhere," fumed Garvin. They were in Garvin's office with the door closed.

"It's about five hundred miles from here. In between Roanoke and Lynchburg," Astrid responded. "It's a very small town. From what I can tell, someone from New York would stand out like a sore thumb. It shouldn't be too hard to find her."

"Ridiculous. There is no way she's happy there. She belongs up here. I can't believe she hasn't come crawling back already," Garvin turned to Astrid. She knew she had to tread carefully.

"Why not just let her be? If she wants to live in some hick town, who cares? Do you really want her back in your life? Remember how unhappy you were when she was here?" Astrid held her breath, waiting for Garvin to explode. She never could tell what would set him off, although Jolene seemed to be a pretty consistent trigger.

Garvin snorted dismissively, "What? You afraid I'll dump you for Jolene? That would be pretty fitting, wouldn't you say? After all, if it wasn't for you, she'd still be here."

"She's gone because you couldn't keep your pants on," snapped Astrid. Noticing Garvin's scowl, she hurriedly continued, "We're both responsible. If I hadn't fallen in love with you…"

"Oh please. Love? You don't know the meaning of the word. Do you really think I'm that stupid? You think you're the first gold-digger I've encountered?" Garvin gave a short laugh. "Let's be clear. You and I have a sexual relationship. Nothing more. You are good in bed, and we look good together. Does that mean this relationship will go further? Of course not. I know if the restaurant fails, you will be gone so fast it will make my head spin. So, you can just cut out the declarations of love. We both know it's bullshit."

"Garvin..." began Astrid.

"What?"

"It's more than that. We make a good team. Admit it. You don't need Jolene, or anybody else. We are good together," Astrid implored.

"That's where you're wrong. Do we look good together? Yes. But, I do need Jolene. Hell, I love Jolene. It doesn't matter how good the sex with you is. I want Jolene back."

Astrid hesitated. "Does this mean we're through?"

Gavin stared at Astrid. "If Jolene agrees to come back, yes, we are through." Neither one said anything for several seconds. Finally, Astrid spoke.

"I guess I better get back to the customers." Garvin watched as she turned and left the office.

Astrid appeared calm, but inside she was in turmoil. This was not working out the way she planned. Garvin was supposed to go after Jolene. When he got there, Jolene would be so distraught that she would either kill herself, or she would threaten Garvin and he would shoot her in self-defense. Then she and Garvin would be together. Now he admitted she was yesterday's news. Astrid also knew that even if Jolene returned, Garvin would get bored again and find someone else. It wouldn't be her. She had to figure out a way to fix this. If Jolene was dead, he would come back to her. Who else could comfort him the way she could? He would be sad for awhile, but then he would get over it. And, she would be back in his life. Astrid sighed. It's like they always say, if you want something done right, you have to do it yourself. Looks like Garvin wouldn't be the only one taking a trip to Virginia.

Marni picked up her phone, started to punch in a number, then hung up and placed the phone back down on the desk. After a moment, she reached for the phone again, but changed her mind and withdrew her hand. She wanted to call Jolene. She was getting more worried every day. Marni knew Garvin would head down to Virginia. Now that he knew where she was, there was no way he would leave her alone. Even though Jolene reassured her that things were under control, Marni knew she was just putting on a brave front. Having seen some of the things Garvin had done to Jolene, she was very concerned. She wondered if she should alert the police down there. Then she dismissed the idea. They would think she was a loony. After all, nothing had actually happened. Marni didn't even know if Garvin was still in New York. Or if he was on the way. Reaching for the phone, she decided she would call the restaurant. She needed to find out if he was there. If he wasn't, then she would call Jolene.

"Garvins," the woman answered.

"May I please speak to Garvin?" Marni asked.

"I'm sorry. You just missed him. Can I help?"

"That's okay. I can call him tomorrow. What time will he be in?"

"I'm afraid starting tomorrow he will be out of town for a few days. Are you sure I can't help you?"

"No, that's fine. I'll try again after he gets back. Thank you." Marni ended the call, then punched in Jolene's number. When Jolene didn't answer, Marni left a message on her voice mail.

"Hey, it's me. Garvin is on his way. I called the restaurant. They said he's out of town for a few days. Please call me as soon as possible! Please be careful! Bye."

Jolene wandered through the aisles, slowly pushing the cart. She was lost in thought about what to make for dinner with Lee. It had to be fairly simple, but she still wanted to impress him. Perusing the meat display, she finally decided on steak. Of course, that also meant mashed potatoes. All she needed was a desert. She loaded the items in her cart, then meandered down the dairy aisle. Cheesecake. She could make a cheesecake. Glancing at her watch, she realized it was later than she thought. Adding the items for the cheesecake, she headed for the checkout. Passing the beer and wine section, she stopped to add a six pack of beer, hoping it was a brand Lee liked. She had a bottle of wine at the house. Somehow, she didn't see Lee as the wine sipping type. Better to stick with the beer. She briefly considered calling him, but then remembered she left the house without her phone. Oh well, it would be fine. She checked out her groceries and headed for the car.

It was late when Jolene got home. She put the groceries away, then took Gunner outside for a little while. Returning to the house, she set about making the cheesecake. By the time she was done with everything, she was exhausted. It was then she remembered her phone. She wandered into the living room, found her phone, noticing the call from Marni. Thinking Marni was calling about the progress on her book, she decided against listening to the voice mail message.

"Sorry Marni. I just don't have the energy tonight. I'll call you tomorrow. Right now, I'm going to take a nice, long shower, then go to bed." She placed the phone back down, then headed upstairs.

CHAPTER FOURTEEN

Lee whistled as he finished getting ready. He was looking forward to the evening with Jolene. When he first met her, he had no idea he would find himself falling for her. Yes, she was attractive, but it was more than that. Originally, he thought a woman from New York City would be snobby and dismissive. On the contrary, he found it easy to imagine she had lived here her whole life. He found they had a lot in common. She loved the outdoors. He felt she truly appreciated nature and the beauty of the area. She was also wickedly funny, once you understood her sense of humor. Lee hoped the dinner would go well. He wanted it to lead to something more. He and his last girlfriend had broken up almost a year ago. He was ready for a new relationship. He knew Jolene was coming off a bad experience with her ex. Hopefully that wouldn't prevent her from wanting to get involved. He reminded himself not to be pushy. Take it slow. He didn't want to blow this opportunity. He checked himself in the mirror. Then picking up the flowers he purchased in town, he headed for the door.

Jolene nervously fussed with her hair. It was humid outside. As usual in the humidity, the layered curls were having a field day. Exasperated, she finally gave her head a final toss, and gave up. Her hair would do what it wanted, no matter what she did. This was as good as it would get. She checked her reflection in the mirror. She decided to go with casual and comfy. Jolene donned a pair of jeans and a dark green top that was offset by her hair color.

She pondered the irony. Not all that long ago, a dinner date with Garvin would mean makeup, hair styled, dress, high heels and jewelry. She looked at the necklace at her throat. The bloodstone shone darkly in the light, standing out against the dark green of her shirt. It was the only piece of jewelry she wore. Somehow, it seemed right. She started to wonder if Rosemary would agree, then laughed as she realized she was worrying about one of her characters. It always amazed her how involved she got with the story and characters when she was writing. During the writing process, they were real. She felt a bit lost when she finished the book. Until the next one.

Even though she and Garvin were through, they had been together a long time. A dinner date with someone else felt weird.

She found she was having a hard time keeping her anxiety at bay. Then, she realized, it was because she cared about Lee. A lot. She did not want to mess this up. He was cute, nice, funny and easy to talk to. She really hoped things would work out between them. Glancing at the clock, she made her way to the kitchen to finish getting the dinner ready. Jolene had decided on steak, mashed potatoes and salad. Keep it simple. Though she did make a cheesecake for dessert. After all, who doesn't like cheesecake?

She finished making the salads, setting them in the refrigerator. Next, she seasoned the steaks with salt, pepper and garlic, then set them aside. She poured a glass of white wine, and sipped while she set the table. Gunner wandered in, looking hopefully at the steaks.

"Don't even consider it," Jolene admonished. "Your food is in the other room. I suggest you go eat it. If you're lucky, there may be leftovers. But, don't bet on it." Gunner sighed and flopped down on the floor under the table. Jolene smiled.

"Suit yourself." She took a final look at the table, then remembered the bread. Quickly, she sliced the loaf of French bread, wrapped it in foil and put it in the toaster oven to warm up. Grabbing the bread basket, she spread a cloth napkin in it.

Once the bread was warm, she placed it in the basket, covering it with the napkin. All those years of hanging out in Garvins paid off. If nothing else, she could set a table. Plus, furnish a bread basket.

Gunner jumped up and sounded the alarm as Lee pulled up the driveway. Jolene went to the door to greet him. She watched him exit the truck, flowers in hand and her heart melted. She smiled broadly, blinking back tears. Garvin would never think to bring flowers. He would leave those details to Astrid. At the thought of Astrid, Jolene felt a pang. Shaking her head, she banished the thought of her past. Not tonight. Tonight, she was going to enjoy herself. Tonight, she begins her new love life. She hoped.

She opened the door. Lee shyly handed her the flowers. Jolene beamed as she thanked him, then found a vase to put them in. Placing the flowers on the table, she turned to Lee.

"What can I get you to drink?" she asked, hand on the refrigerator door.

"I'll take a beer if you have it," Lee answered.

"Sure thing." Jolene fetched the beer and a glass, handing both to Lee. "I hope you like steak and potatoes."

"I love steak and potatoes. And everything smells great," Lee smiled.

Jolene was nervous. She wanted everything to be perfect. They sat at the table, and she served the food. Lee ate heartily complimenting her cooking. Jolene felt her stress melting away. Lee was low key, proving easy to be with. He regaled her with stories of growing up in rural Virginia. She found herself laughing more than she had in years. She felt comfortable with him. She realized she hadn't felt that way in a very long time.

"Have you finished the book yet?" Lee inquired.

"Not yet. After what you told me about the prior owners, I decided to do some research. I called the real estate agency to talk to the agent who sold me the house. I figured he would know the history. Turns out, he killed himself."

"What?!" Lee was shocked.

"Yeah. It was quite a shock for everyone. Anyway, a woman from the office met me later on. She told me all these stories about how everyone who lives here either dies, or moves away. She is blaming Dale's death on the house."

"How can she blame the house?" Lee scoffed.

"I know. But, it got me thinking of everything I've experienced. I know some may be vermin or snakes, but I haven't told you everything that has happened. I think there may be some truth to those rumors." Jolene paused a moment. "You think I'm crazy, don't you?"

Lee smiled, "Nah. But I am a bit concerned. You said that woman is convinced the house killed people. Let's say the house is haunted. What if there is something to what she told you? Maybe it's not safe for you to be here."

"I don't know if I'd go that far," Jolene responded. "I'll admit some of the things have freaked me out a bit. But, I'm hoping there is a reasonable explanation. I'll tell you something that is rather odd. Or maybe it's just my imagination. I don't know."

"What is it?"

Jolene hesitated. "You may think I'm loony for sure after this, but, it's the book. I've written a bunch of books. I get inspired by various things, and the creativity just flows. However, in this case, it's almost like something else is leading me on this one. I almost feel like it's not me doing the writing. Like, someone, or something else, is telling the story."

"You mean like Patience Worth?" Lee asked.

Jolene stared, mouth open. "How in the world do you know about Patience Worth?"

"I saw a program about it on TV," Lee blushed. "Of course, who knows if it's true or not. It was pretty compelling. I mean, here is a woman from the early nineteen hundreds, barely educated, who had never been out of the country, and yet, she's writing a book in a different type of language. And she describes places she has never been. All supposedly told to her by a ghost named Patience Worth."

"Lee, you totally amaze me," she laughed, "I actually tried to read one of the books. I couldn't get through it. The language was just too difficult. So maybe it was written by a ghost from another century. Who knows?"

"Well, maybe you have your own Patience Worth helping out," laughed Lee.

"If it helps me write, fine. Especially, since I'm in a bit of a quandary right now."

"How so?" asked Lee.

"Well, it's looking like I'm going to kill off my main characters, which could be a problem," laughed Jolene. "I guess between all the weird things I've been experiencing in the house and the issues with my ex, I am being a little rough on my poor characters. But, like I said, I'm in the middle of the story, so things can change. I can add more characters, or I can save the ones I have. It all depends on how the story speaks to me, what direction it takes."

"That doesn't sound good. Did you put your ex in the wall?"

"Not exactly," laughed Jolene. "Someone is going in the wall, but not him. I was thinking Garvin's character might die in a car accident."

"Remind me to stay on your good side," laughed Lee, a bit timorously.

Jolene smiled back, "You don't have to worry. You're on my good side. Hell, maybe I'll have a nice contractor show up and rescue the woman in the wall."

"You know us contractors. We're always looking to rescue a damsel in distress," Lee smiled again.

"That's good to know. I may have to take you up on that someday." Jolene's smile faded slightly. "I've heard Garvin, my ex, may be headed this way. It could be nothing, or depending on his mood and consumption of alcohol, it could be something else entirely."

Lee was suddenly serious, "Will he hurt you? Do you need me to be here? I don't want anything to happen to you." Jolene felt her heart skip a beat. His concern was palpable. She knew Lee would protect her if she asked. But, at the same time, she wanted to be strong. She didn't want to have to rely on a man to take care of her.

"I don't know. I hate to dump this on you, especially tonight. But, you should know what you are getting involved in. Garvin is…complicated. He can be verbally abusive. I'll admit, there were some pretty heated battles. Would he hurt me? It's a possibility. But, if he isn't drinking, or in one of his moods, he may be civil. I'm sure he just wants me back because I left him. Garvin hates to lose. Once I explain I'm not going back, maybe he will just go back home."

"Jolene. This doesn't sound like something to try to handle alone. Do you know when he is coming?"

"No. All I know, is that he knows where I am. Who knows? Maybe he won't even show up. Maybe he'll decide it's not worth the time." Jolene prayed that was true. She didn't want Lee upset. "Listen. It's not like I'm not prepared. I have Gunner."

"Gunner is fine. Maybe that will help. But, I'm going to be here. I won't butt in if you don't want me to, but I'm here to help," Lee said solemnly.

"Thank you, Lee. I really appreciate that," Jolene said.

Lee smiled. "Good.

Now that we got that settled, didn't you say there was cheesecake?"

CHAPTER FIFTEEN

Professor Rupert Kozmo listened to the message on his phone. It was from a woman, with a New York accent. He rolled his eyes. Another city person moves to the country, buys an old house, hears noises and assumes it's haunted. Sighing, he sipped his drink. He had responded to this type of call in the past. He would show up and find nothing. Generally, it was mice or squirrels, or even raccoons in the attic. Of course, the people that called him out didn't want to hear that. They would insist the place was haunted. They would call him a fraud. Or worse. *It was all these damn ghost hunter shows on TV,* he thought, annoyed. People watch them, then they think every little creak in the house is paranormal.

He toyed with the idea of not returning the call. The last thing he wanted to do was go on another wild goose chase. Except there was something different about this call. The woman told him Janice gave her his number. He had a feeling he knew what house she was talking about. Ice clinked as he took another sip of his drink. Did he want to get involved in this one? He had to admit, if that was the house, he was curious. He wasn't immune to the rumor mill. This one might actually be worth his time. He stared out the window for several more moments. Then picked up the phone and placed the call.

Jolene hung up and pondered the phone call. It had taken the better part of the morning to get up the nerve to use the number Janice had given her. She felt silly enough calling Rupert. Stammering like a fool probably didn't help. Rupert had been haughty and a bit arrogant, unnerving her. Jolene found herself feeling like a school girl again. She learned he taught English at a local college. If she felt like this after one phone call, she could only imagine what his students felt like. Feeling like she failed an exam, Jolene was surprised when Rupert agreed to come out to the house. She was relieved, but also anxious. He had been intimidating enough on the phone. What would he be like in person? What the hell had she just gotten herself into?

She glanced at the unread voicemail from Marni. Jolene sighed. She felt guilty not calling back. After all, Marni was her friend.

"I'm sorry Marni. I'll call back soon. I promise. I just can't handle any more pressure right now. The book will get done when it gets done."

Jolene went to the kitchen, fixed a snack and glass of tea, then with resignation, opened her laptop and began to write.

Rosemary finished feeding the pigs. She glanced over at the dog sitting quietly nearby.

"At least this time you didn't have to rescue me," she said. "But I'm sure glad you are here. Just in case." Gathering up the food buckets, she headed to the barn, the dog following at her heels. She put away the buckets and made sure everything was in order. The cows were out in the field, grazing. For now, her chores were done. She glanced at the sky. Not a cloud to be seen. It was still early morning, but the temperature was rising. It was going to be a scorcher. Rosemary decided she needed to head to town and get the shopping done before the heat became unbearable.

Bobby watched as Rosemary drove away. He knew she was going to the store. But, he also was sure she was going to see a boyfriend. No amount of denials would convince him otherwise. He was going to have to teach her a lesson. He looked over and watched as the dog lay down in the shade of the barn. Bobby resented the dog. It was another mouth to feed they couldn't afford. But, she wouldn't listen. Here he was, working his ass off trying to keep them afloat and she adds the dog. The heat of the morning making him angry, his resentment finally boiled over. He was going to set things right, once and for all. Bobby stormed into the house and got his gun.

Rosemary was in the attic. She reread the latest letter, then slowly put it back in its hiding place. She fingered the necklace at her throat. The feeling of dread that woke her this morning was still with her, only stronger. Bobby was becoming more unstable. It frightened her. His constant harangues about money were wearing her down. She was already pinching pennies as much as possible. She looked down at her clothes. They were worn and fraying. She had patched them numerous times, until she couldn't patch them anymore. She saw the looks of pity from other women when she went into town. It was a small town. Everyone knew everyone else's business. It was embarrassing, but Rosemary knew Bobby would have a fit if she bought anything new.

She didn't like the way he stared at the necklace. It would only be a matter of time before he demanded she sell it. Unless… A thought came to her. He couldn't sell it if she didn't have it. Removing the necklace, she gently placed it in the hiding hole with the letters. Wiping tears from her eyes, she carefully closed the hole, making sure it was virtually invisible. Dejectedly, she stood up, and went downstairs.

"Have you seen the dog?" she asked Bobby. "I haven't seen him in a few days."

"Nope. Maybe he went back where he came from." Bobby kept working on the tractor.

Rosemary looked around. "Maybe, but I just feel like something is wrong."

"It's just a damn dog!" Bobby yelled. "It was a stray. That's what they do. They show up. Then they run off. Quit worrying about it and give me a hand here!" Rosemary fell silent, handing Bobby the wrench he pointed to. They worked in silence, punctuated only by Bobby's curses. Finally, they were finished. Bobby wiped his hands on his coveralls. Rosemary sat quietly, staring out the barn door. Bobby shook his head.

"Fine. If the damn dog means that much to you, we can go look for him." Rosemary's face lit up.

"Oh Bobby, thank you! I know you think he's just a dumb dog, but he does mean a lot to me," she cried. Jumping up, she put her arms around Bobby. "Thank you."

Bobby held her briefly, then let her go. "Well, let's go have a look." They started walking out the door, when he stopped and turned to look at Rosemary. "Where is that necklace of yours? How come you're not wearing it?"

Rosemary flushed, then stammered, her hand instinctively going to her throat.

"I, ugh, I...Oh Bobby, I think I may have lost it!" Breaking into tears, she looked beseechingly up at her husband. "Please don't be mad! I've looked everywhere, but I can't find it! I'm so afraid it's lost!" She prayed he would believe her, even if it meant incurring his wrath. She swore she would never reveal where the necklace was.

"Damn it woman! How many times have I told you to be careful! That necklace might be the only thing that saves us from starvation! You better find it, you hear me?!" Bobby glared at his wife.

"Yes, I know. I'll find it! It has to be here somewhere," she sobbed. Bobby looked at her with disgust.

"Quit crying already. Go look for the damn dog. Maybe you'll find the necklace, too."

Later that evening, as she finished cleaning up after dinner, Rosemary heard Bobby yell.

"I found him! I found that damn dog!"

"Where?!" she cried, running to the other room. Stopping in the middle of the room, she looked around, puzzled. "Bobby? Where are you?"

"In here. In the closet," he responded. Curiously, Rosemary stepped towards the open closet. Peeking in, she looked to the right, and saw Bobby standing near something on the floor. It was the dog.

"How did he get in here? Is he okay?" she clambered her way in the closet, squeezing past Bobby, kneeling next to the dog. "Oh Bobby, I think he's dead!" she cried. Suddenly, she noticed the wound. It was a bullet hole. The reality of what had happened hit her like a ton of bricks. Years of abuse by her husband welled up. She jumped up, spinning to face him.

"You son of a bitch!! You killed him!! I hate you!!" she screamed. She swung her fist, connecting to his face. "I HATE YOU! I HOPE YOU DIE, YOU BASTARD!"

Bobby roared with rage at the blow, eyes filled with hate. Despite her own rage, Rosemary noticed the utter blackness in his eyes, but it was too late. Bobby smashed his fist against the side of her head. She fell back, landing with a thud on the floor, unconscious. Bobby stood breathing hard for several moments. Satisfied she wasn't getting up, he backed up and pulled the piece of plywood that had been propped against the wall. Moving it into place, he sealed up the space where Rosemary lay with the dog's body. Picking up the hammer and nails hidden nearby, he proceeded to nail the plywood in place.

"You'll listen to me, now, won't you, bitch. You aren't coming out until I say so, you hear me?!" he yelled. He violently kicked the plywood, not even making a dent. "Just try to get out of there. I'm in

99

control now." Satisfied, he left the closet and closed the door.

Bobby staggered a bit as he headed for the truck. He could imagine Rosemary screaming his name and banging on the walls. He knew she would panic. Let her suffer for a bit, the useless whore. Showing off everything she had to all the men in town. This would teach her. She would be glad to see him whenever he decided to let her out of the closet. But for now, let her stay with that miserable cur she took in. Bobby laughed out loud remembering the expression on her face when she saw the dead dog. Next time, she'll listen when he said no more animals.

He slid behind the wheel of the truck, dropping the keys on the floor. Cursing, he bent down and fumbled around until he recovered them. Trying to put the key in the ignition, he dropped it again. He cursed some more, then once again recovered the key. Starting the engine, he put the truck in gear and headed down the driveway.

The night was dark, clouds blocking any light from the moon as he drove along. He opened another can of beer and took a long swig. The truck weaved a bit back and forth as he drove along. This section of the road was curvy, with deep ditches on either side. It was notorious for being a dangerous section. Every year, someone was badly injured or died in an accident. Usually, they took one of the turns too fast, and lost control. Sometimes, deer would jump out, causing the drivers to swerve off the side into the ditch.

Bobby wasn't feeling threatened by the road however. Tonight, he knew he was invincible. He was King of his house, Lord of the manor. Nothing was going to stop him. Not tonight, or any other night. He started to think of how contrite Rosemary would be when he got back. She would beg his forgiveness and offer to do anything he wanted. He felt a stirring in his groin at what he would make her do. He smiled, finished the beer and tossed the can out the window. He was still smiling when the dog appeared in the road. It took a moment to get through Bobby's alcohol-soaked brain, but then he stopped smiling, mouth open, eyes wide. It was the dog he shot and put in the closet! Standing in the middle of the road, teeth bared.

Before Bobby could react, the dog leapt forward, onto the hood of the truck, snarling and snapping. Bobby screamed, yanking the wheel hard to the left. The truck shot across the road, into the ditch. Bouncing high, the force of the impact causing the truck to roll several times upon landing, before crashing into a tree. Not wearing a seat belt, Bobby was ejected from the truck like a rag doll. He plopped down directly in the path when the truck started to roll. He was already dying when the truck burst into flames.

Rosemary groggily opened her eyes. It only took a moment before she remembered her predicament. Panicked, she scrambled to her feet, bumping into the walls. The space was just barely big enough for her to stand. Turning around required finesse. Her heart was galloping, and she wondered if she was having a heart attack. How could he do this to her? He knew she hated being in small, cramped spaces. Sweat poured off her body. Tears flooded her eyes. He wouldn't let her die in here. Or would he? No, he had to come back. He just had to. She looked down at the lifeless body of the dog at her feet. Bobby shot the dog because she cared about it. What if he had lost all touch with reality? What if he never came back? Fear paralyzed her. Suddenly, she started screaming. Banging on the walls, she tried to find a way out.

She worked her way around the small space but was unable to find any way to break out. Exhausted, hands bloody and battered, she slowly sank back down on the floor. It was then she remembered her angry last words. I hate you, she had said. I hope you die. Now a new fear came over her. She thought about all the times she lay in bed, wishing he would die in a car wreck, or farm accident. What if it *happened now? He was drunk when he left. What if she got her wish? Isn't that the old saying? Be careful what you wish for. The realization was overwhelming: she was going to die in here. She buried her face in her hands, shoulders shaking with her sobs, and wept.*

CHAPTER SIXTEEN

Astrid drove through New Jersey, being careful not to speed. She did not want to give the cops any reason to pull her over. Not that she was worried about getting a ticket. She knew she could charm her way out of most anything, at least with the male cops. It was the gun in the glove box that concerned her. She knew she couldn't carry a gun from New York into New Jersey. If she was stopped, they would find the gun and she would be in deep doo doo. She kept glancing in her rear-view mirror, on the lookout for any troopers.

Once she was out of New Jersey, she breathed a little easier. She would still need to be cautious, but knew it wouldn't be quite as bad. She had left New York ahead of Garvin and hoped to get to Jolene's house before he showed up.

Astrid still wasn't quite sure what her plan was. She had several options in her head, though none of them were foolproof. She had a feeling she was going to have to get Jolene to attack her, in which case Astrid could shoot and claim self-defense. The details would need to be ironed out before she actually got to the house. She would have to come up with a reason for being there. Perhaps she could say Jolene called and begged her to come down to try and work things out. But what about Garvin? Maybe she could say she was worried about what Jolene would do to him. That's why she was there. That might work. At any rate, she still had a long way to travel. Plenty of time to figure it out.

Garvin stopped at the gas station. He wasn't used to sitting in a car this long and needed to get out and stretch. After filling the tank, he went into the convenience store and bought a drink

and some snacks. Part of him was wondering why he was doing
this. Maybe he should just call Jolene and talk to her. He had only
been on the road for a few hours. He still had a long way to go.
What he was discovering about driving for such a long time was
that it gave him too much time to think.

At first, he imagined he would show up, talk sense into
Jolene, then bring her home. The longer he drove, the more he
thought about it. She had been gone for several months now and
hadn't called. Not once. No texts, nothing. He had tried calling,
but she must have blocked his number. Initially, the thought that
she might not want to come home never entered his mind. He
knew if he showed up, apologized about Astrid, swore it would
never happen again, she would forgive him and come home. For
the first time, a niggle of doubt entered his mind. Could it be
possible she wouldn't forgive him? Could she really want to stay
in Virginia? Garvin shook the doubt from his mind. She's had her
fun. Now it was time to get back to normal.

Jolene wiped the sweat from her face. The air was thick
and humid, making It hard to breathe. The wind was picking up,
a storm was on the way. Glancing towards the west, she saw the
darkening of the clouds.

"Come on Gunner. Let's go inside before we get rained
on." The storm was predicted to be pretty severe. A few large rain
drops fell, and Jolene hurried to the back door. Opening the door,
Gunner shot past her into the house.

"Hey! Ladies first!" she laughed. They had just entered the
house when the storm let loose with a fury. Rain came down in
sheets, while the wind roared. Jolene looked out the window,
seeing only dark sky, the rain now blowing sideways. The house
shook with each boom of thunder, making her jump. The

lightning flared, lighting the sky briefly, before it all turned dark again.

"Holy shit!" Jolene yelled. The rain pounded on the metal roof, unnerving her. She could barely hear herself think. Gunner whined, pacing from room to room restlessly. Jolene stood in the middle of the living room, unsure what to do. She knew with the lightning that she should stay away from the windows. If this storm turned even more violent, she should probably stay in the center of the house. It was then she heard it. In the ceiling, directly above her head. Scratching noises. Loud enough to be heard above the cacophony of the storm. Jolene stared at the ceiling. The scratching stopped, then she heard something else. Thumping. It sounded as if someone was walking around in her bedroom.

"Oh, come on! Not now!" She glanced from the ceiling to Gunner. The big dog had stopped whining. He was intently watching the ceiling, following the sound of the footsteps. Jolene didn't know what to do. Was someone in the house? She had gotten into the habit of not locking the doors while she was outside. What if someone snuck in? What if it was Garvin? She glanced around for anything that could be used as a weapon. Not seeing anything worthwhile, she called to Gunner.

"Come on. We'll go up together. You'll just have to protect me." Taking hold of Gunner's collar, she led the dog to the stairs. Gunner paused, then suddenly shot up the stairs, growling. When he reached the top of the stairs, he turned and ran to the bedroom, barking. Jolene hesitated at the bottom of the stairs, fully expecting to see someone run out the room. Gunner was huge and intimidating. Especially when he was barking and growling like he was doing now.

When no one came out of the room, Jolene slowly started up the stairs. She reached the top. She had just turned to head down the hallway, when she felt ice-cold air surround her. Wrapping her arms around herself, she shivered. Gunner came out of the bedroom, stopping in the doorway. He stared at her, not coming any closer. He whined again. He seemed confused about something as he watched her.

Then, just as suddenly as it appeared, the cold air dissipated. Jolene felt warmth return to her body. Gunner noticed, too. He walked up to Jolene, sniffed her, then sat down. Jolene looked towards the bedroom. She waited several moments, then slowly walked to the door. Looking in the room, she could clearly see there was no one there. She jumped when thunder and lightning exploded outside the window.

"It has to be mice. Or maybe a big-ass snake. It just seems like a ghost or something because of the storm," Jolene said nervously. Despite trying to a strong, independent woman, she had to admit, she was freaking out. Something was going on. As much as she'd like to believe somehow it was vermin in the attic or walls, her gut told her it was something else. She would have to figure out how to deal with whatever it was. She didn't know how dangerous it was. She just hoped she would survive.

CHAPTER SEVENTEEN

Lee was feeling uneasy. The dinner date had gone well. He was looking forward to the next one. Today he was on call for the rescue squad. Lately, things had been pretty quiet. He was hoping today would be another quiet one. However, he had a feeling that wasn't going to be the case. He didn't know why, but he couldn't shake the uneasiness. Maybe it was the storm. Maybe it was the talk about Garvin coming down. He wanted to call Jolene. He wanted to hang out at her place. He could run calls from there. Plus, he would be there if Garvin did show up. Except, Jolene might get insulted, thinking he needed to protect her. He knew how independent she was. But, he couldn't help himself. He was worried. *What the hell. It won't hurt to call and ask if she wants some company,* he thought. Before he could dial her number, his pager went off. Lee listened to the dispatcher: motor vehicle accident, one injury. Sighing, he put his phone back, radioed in his response, then headed for the crew station to pick up the ambulance.

"How the hell does anyone drive on these roads?" Astrid was battling the storm, trying to keep the car on the road. In the pouring rain, it was difficult to tell where the edge of the road was. She had cars riding her bumper, adding to her agitation. "Who the fuck wants to live out here? This is ridiculous!" She glared as the driver behind her pulled around to pass. "Jesus! I can't believe they drive like this down here!" Carefully, well below the speed limit, she followed her GPS until she got to the road Jolene lived on. Finding an area that looked like an abandoned driveway, she pulled over. She needed time to get her thoughts together. Calm her nerves. She could just make out Jolene's driveway up ahead. Astrid hadn't counted on how long the driveway was. She could barely make out the house behind some trees. Astrid would stand out like a sore thumb. If Jolene was looking out the window, would see her coming. She needed to figure out how to sneak in.

Garvin was also having issues navigating the roads in the storm. The longer he drove, the more he cursed Jolene for leaving him. *This is all her fault,* he thought. *If she had just let him explain. If she hadn't run off half-cocked, he wouldn't be risking life and limb driving in this mess. If I wanted to drive, I wouldn't have moved to the city. And now I've left the business alone, and I'm driving God knows where, in some hellacious, God awful storm. This is pissing me off! Just wait till I get ahold of her,* he thought, his anger building. *She is definitely going to pay for this.*

Jolene listened to the thunder as it rattled the old house. Gunner paced nervously, whining. Every so often, he would stop, and tilt his head, as if listening to something only he could hear. Suddenly, he ran to the windows, jumping up on the couch so he could stare out, growling.

"What is it?" Jolene asked, but the big dog just continued to stare. After several tense moments, he jumped off the couch, trotting out of the room to start his patrol of the house once again. Something was going on. She could feel it. It was making Jolene nervous. Gunner normally didn't act this way, even in storms. Her imagination started to run wild. What if there was a bear or something out there? She knew they were in the area. Cougars had also been reported nearby, though no officials would admit they were in the area. Or, what if it was a murderer? Almost as bad, or possibly even worse, what if it was whatever was in the house? While researching the paranormal, she found numerous claims that the paranormal fed off energy. This storm had energy in spades. Another boom of thunder, combined with a brilliant flash of lightening, made her jump. The storm was now directly overhead.

Astrid checked the weather again. The storm was an incredibly slow moving one. She looked out at how dark it was. It was then she realized she could probably drive up the driveway with her lights off. In the dark of the storm, she might not be seen. She would need to find a place to hide the car, then sneak into the house. She looked down at her phone, studying the map of the property that she had pulled up earlier. She wanted to memorize the layout before she continued.

Garvin turned onto Crab Apple Road, peering intently through the windshield, looking for Jolene's driveway. He barely registered the car parked on the side of the road. Not paying any attention to it, he kept driving. He was consumed with thoughts of what lay ahead. He almost missed the driveway, slamming on the brakes in order to make the turn. A rush of adrenaline coursed through his body as he drove up the driveway. The hunt was almost over. He smiled thinking of Jolene's reaction when she saw him. She would be like a scared, cornered rabbit. He knew she would give up and agree to go back with him. She would have no choice.

Lee pulled up to the wreck, parking the ambulance in front of the state trooper. The red lights of the ambulance flashed alongside the blue strobe lights of the trooper's car. The rain continued its steady pour. Lee pulled the hood up of his rain jacket as he got out of the ambulance. It was a single car accident. The car had hydroplaned off the road into a tree. Fortunately, the driver hadn't been going that fast. The airbags and seat belts did their job. The driver, a young woman, was shaken up and bruised. She didn't appear to have any serious injuries. Lee and the other crew member stayed with the driver. They talked to her in an effort to calm her down, assess her injuries. Only then would they determine if she needed transport to the hospital. The woman requested they call her mother, refusing any treatment until her mother got on scene. Lee looked at his partner and shrugged. They would be there awhile.

Gunner jumped up and ran to the window, barking furiously. Jolene followed him, peering out in the dark and rain. Headlights illuminated the driveway. *Who the hell would be showing up at her house, especially in this weather?* She wondered. Taking hold of Gunner's collar, she led him to the door. Whoever it was, they would have to get past Gunner first. After the welcome lady, the only other person that had come out to the house was Lee. Everyone in town was convinced the place was haunted, or bad luck, so it was unlikely anyone would just show up. Then it hit her.

"Oh shit. He's here," she said. Her anxiety kicked into overdrive. She fervently wished Lee was here for support. She stood at the door, holding Gunner's collar, watching the car pull slowly around the back and park. Her heart skipped a beat when she saw Garvin get out. Emotions flooded through her. Despite everything, the sight of him stirred something in her. She realized that she still cared. Maybe not a lot, but if she thought she had banished him from her heart, she was mistaken. Then, almost as quickly, she remembered the last time she saw him. In her bed with Astrid. Her heart hardened again. She could do this. Whatever he wanted, it didn't matter. She would tell him to get back in his car and go back where he came from.

Gunner stopped barking, staring intently as Garvin approached the door. A low growl emanated from his throat.

"Easy," Jolene told him, quietly. She could feel her knees shaking. She steeled herself as she watched him approach. Garvin stopped when he saw her standing in the doorway. His eyes went from Jolene to Gunner, then back to Jolene.

"What are you doing here?" Jolene's voice was icy.

"Nice to see you, too. Why do you think I'm here? We need to talk," Garvin replied, matching her tone.

"There is nothing to talk about. So, you can just hop back in your car and leave."

"Jolene. I've just driven nine hours, the last hour in a storm, to talk to you. At least let me come in out of the damn rain and talk. If you still want me to leave, fine. But you can do me the courtesy of hearing me out." Garvin waited while Jolene thought it over. Without a word, she held the door open, then backed away, still holding onto Gunner's collar.

"Does he bite?" Garvin asked as he entered the kitchen.

"All dogs bite," Jolene replied. "Okay, you're here. Now talk."

Garvin glanced around the kitchen, not bothering to hide his disdain.

"I can't believe you live here. What a dump."

"If you came here to insult me, you may as well turn

around now," Jolene snapped. "This is my house. You don't need to insult me, or my house. Try to pretend you have some class and manners."

"Sorry," Garvin said. "Look. I know you're upset about what happened. I'm here to say it's over between me and Astrid. I want you back, Jolene. I'm sorry I hurt you. Please. Come home."

Jolene's heart was racing. All those nights she cried herself to sleep, wishing to hear exactly what she was now hearing. Oh, how she had wanted to hear those words. She would have believed him. She would have returned and given it another try. But now, time had passed. Now, she was learning to be on her own. Now, there was Lee.

"No."

"What do you mean, no? Think about it. Think about what we had. You can't be happy here!" Garvin waved his hand around the room. "Look at this place! You're in the middle of nowhere!"

"I am thinking about what we had! And I'm also thinking of how you so cruelly and easily threw it all away!" Jolene yelled. "So, you're not with Astrid anymore, big fucking deal. There will be another one, I'm sure. I can't trust you anymore! Don't you get it?"

"Stop it, that's not true! I love you, Jolene! I swear, if you come back, we'll start over. Just you and me. It will be like old times," Garvin responded, trying hard not to sound like he was begging.

"Bullshit!" Before either of them could say anything else, Gunner turned towards the door and barked. Both Garvin and Jolene stared in disbelief. Standing in the doorway, looking like a drowned rat, dripping water all over the floor, was Astrid.

"What the fuck are you doing here?!" yelled Garvin.

"I can't believe this shit," Jolene muttered, gripping

Gunner's collar tighter. "What do you want Astrid?"

"Well, isn't this cozy," Astrid replied nonchalantly.

"Okay, that's it. I want both of you out of here. Now! Go away and leave me alone!" Jolene made a move towards Astrid.

"Stop right there!" Astrid yelled. Pulling a gun out of her coat, she pointed it at Jolene.

"Astrid, are you crazy?! Put that down before you hurt someone!" yelled Garvin. He brushed aside Jolene and strode towards Astrid.

"Garvin, stay out of this," Astrid said, turning the gun on him. "This is between me and Jolene. But, I will shoot you if you don't back off. I mean it!"

"Astrid, you're crazy! Put the gun down!" Garvin yelled, but didn't move closer.

Astrid looked first at Garvin, then Jolene, then back to Garvin. She smiled. "I heard you, you know. How you're through with me. When exactly did that happen? After we had sex this morning, before you left to come here?"

"Astrid…" Garvin glared, "I'm warning you…"

"Be serious," she scoffed. "What are you going to do? Dump me? According to what I just heard, that's already a done deal. So what?" What are you going to do?" Garvin started towards Astrid.

"I said stop! Or do you want to get shot?" she challenged. Garvin stopped again. "I thought so. Now, that we are all here together, what are we going to do?" she asked. "How are we going to resolve this?"

"You can both leave right now," replied Jolene. "I am done with both of you. If you have an issue with Garvin, I suggest you take it outside. I don't want to see either of you ever again."

Astrid turned the gun back to Jolene. "How about I just

shoot you? Maybe even both of you? Isn't that what you said once? How does it feel now? How do you like having a gun pointed at you?"

"Astrid. I'm telling you, put the damn gun down," Garvin said sternly. Astrid only smiled again. The smile didn't reach her eyes, which were dark and cold. "You know, I've had about enough of you, too." She swung the gun back to Garvin, just as Gunner launched himself forward. Astrid moved too late. Gunner's teeth sank into her arm. She screamed, the gun going off with a deafening boom as she fell to the floor. She lay there stunned for a moment. Then, realizing what she had just done, Astrid wasted no time as she scrambled to her feet and ran out the door.

The young woman driver finally decided not to go to the hospital. Lee and his partner, Joe, finished the paperwork. Climbing into the ambulance, they heard the call go off for a shooting. Lee's heart stopped for a second when he heard the address. It was Jolene's house. Picking up the mic, he radioed in that they were responding. Joe barely had time to shut the door, let alone fasten his seat belt, when Lee pulled back out onto the road.

"Hey, easy! We don't even know if the scene is secure yet," he told Lee.

"I know. Hopefully we'll have more info before we get there," Lee responded. They both listened intently to the radio, as the dispatcher relayed information to the responding deputies. The ambulance was speeding along, when a car flew past them.

"Idiot!" shouted Joe. "She's going to end up being our next call, driving like that in the rain!"

"Let's hope not. I think we have our hands full as it is,"

Lee said. He reached Jolene's road. He noticed the blue lights of the deputies ahead. Keying the mic, he told dispatch they were almost on scene. The dispatcher relayed for them to stage at the bottom of the driveway, until the deputies advised the scene was safe. Lee pulled into the bottom of the driveway, anxiously waiting for the okay to proceed. After what seemed like an eternity, they were finally given the okay. Lee drove quickly up the driveway, parking next to one of the patrol cars. He and Joe leaped out. They ran to the back of the ambulance. Throwing the back doors open, they quickly put the backboard on the stretcher, along with the oxygen and trauma bag. Stretcher in tow, both raced into the house. Lee's heart was in his throat. They still had no idea who was shot, or how badly.

Lee entered the house first, Joe on his heels. There were several deputies in the small kitchen. Lee saw someone on the ground, bleeding. He pushed his way to the patient, realizing it was a man. Jolene kneeled next to the him, holding a towel to the wound on his stomach.

"Garvin, hang on. Help is here." Garvin lay with his eyes closed, not responding. Jolene looked up at Lee, eyes wide. "Lee, thank God. I think he's going into shock," she said. Lee and Joe knelt down next to Garvin. Joe set up the oxygen, placing the mask on Garvin's face. Lee began cutting away Garvin's shirt, to examine the wound. There was an entry wound on the left side of Garvin's stomach.

"Are you okay?" he asked her.

"Yes, I'm fine. And I'm really glad to see you," she smiled shakily.

"Me too. Joe, hand me the large trauma dressing." Lee opened the bandage, and carefully placed it over the wound, securing it in place. Joe, meanwhile, checked Garvin's vital signs.

"Bp is 90 over 70, pulse 100 and thready," Joe reported. He swiftly prepared the IV bag, then handed the catheter to Lee, who deftly inserted it into Garvin's arm.

"Let's roll him over, look for an exit wound," Lee said. They quickly rolled Garvin on his right side, checking for signs of an exit wound. While they had him on his side, they slid the backboard underneath him.

"Right there," Joe said, pointing to a wound on Garvin's back. "Hang on, let me put this dressing on it." Joe quickly opened the bandage and covered the wound. "Okay, done. We need to get going."

They eased Garvin back down on the backboard, strapped him to the board and lifted him onto the stretcher. Gathering up their equipment, they hustled Garvin out of the house. Soon they had him loaded into the ambulance. Jolene followed close behind. Joe jumped in the front to drive, Lee was in the back with Garvin. Jolene poked her head in the door.

"I'm going to follow you," she said.

"Okay, but don't run any lights or anything. Please. I don't want to see anything happen to you," Lee said as he quickly hooked Garvin up to the EKG machine. He switched the oxygen tubing from the portable tank to the on-board unit. "I'll talk to you once we get there. We need to roll."

"Okay." Jolene closed the ambulance door, watching as it headed down the driveway. After filling the police in on what had happened, she let them know she was heading to the hospital, got in her car, and headed out.

By the time Jolene arrived at the hospital, Garvin was being evaluated in the emergency room. The bullet had missed all the major organs. It had gone clean through his body with minimal damage. He was in pain, and would need time to heal, but he was lucky. The doctor was with Garvin, so Jolene tracked down Lee, who was in a small room off the ER, filling out the incident report. When he saw her, he jumped up and hugged her.

"I was so worried when I heard the call. I was so afraid you had gotten shot. What happened?" Lee asked.

"Oh my God. I was so scared. First, Garvin shows up. We get into an argument. I basically tell him it's over. I tell him to leave. He starts talking about how it's over with Astrid, he wants me back, blah, blah, blah. Next thing I know, Astrid is standing in the doorway with a gun. She gets into it with Garvin. I guess she didn't like that he was dumping her. Anyway, next thing I know, Gunner attacks Astrid, and the gun went off. I still can't believe this all happened."

"I'm so glad you're okay," Lee said. "What happened to Astrid? I didn't hear if the cops got her or not."

"I don't know. She took off running. As far as I know, she hasn't been found yet. They know who she is. And where she lives. If the cops here don't get her, they'll get her in New York."

"What if she comes back?" Lee asked worriedly.

"I don't think she will. Not with Gunner. He did a number on her arm. I'm surprised she isn't here at the hospital."

"I'm sure she won't stop anywhere near here. She has to know the cops will check all the local hospitals for a woman with dog bites. But, I'll still be glad when I hear she's been caught."

"Yeah, me too. Have you heard how Garvin is? Is he ok?"

"He got lucky. The bullet didn't hit any major organs. He doesn't even need surgery. I'm sure he'll be staying overnight, maybe a day or two. Then they will release him."

"That's good. Even with everything that happened, I don't want to see him die. Not anymore, anyway," Jolene smiled.

"Well, at least you probably have some good material for your book," joked Lee.

"You know it. This one will be a doozy." Then turning serious again, she added, "Do you think Astrid is really gone? I hadn't really thought about her, but now you have me wondering if I will be ok at home."

"I don't know. If you want, I can always stay with you," offered Lee. Jolene looked into his eyes.

"I would like that. Very much."

"Okay then. I'll finish up here and come over after I drop off the ambulance. How does that sound?"

"That sounds great. I'm just going to stop in and be sure Garvin is okay. I want him to understand what happened doesn't change anything. I'm not going back to New York. Then I'll head home and wait for you," Jolene answered, relief evident in her voice.

"Sounds like a plan," Lee smiled. Taking her face in his hands, he gently kissed her. "I'll see you after a while."

"Okay. See you later," Jolene said, smiling.

Garvin's eyes were closed when she entered the room. He looked terrible. Jolene felt a stab of sympathy seeing how pale he was. This was not the Garvin she knew. She moved closer to the bed.

"Hey," she said softly. Garvin's eyelids fluttered, then opened. It took him several moments to get oriented.

"What happened?" he asked groggily. "Where am I?" He tried sitting up, but Jolene stopped him.

"Take it easy. You're in the hospital. You've been shot," she said.

"You shot me?" Garvin's eyes widened.

"No, of course not! Astrid shot you. The doctors say you're lucky to be alive. She could have killed you," Jolene retorted.

"Astrid? What is she doing here? Where is she?" Despite Jolene's protestations, Garvin managed to sit up.

"No one knows. She took off after the shooting. She could be anywhere."

"Oh my God."

"Listen. I just wanted to check on you before I go. I'm pretty sure you will be released in a couple of days. I can call the restaurant and tell them what happened. Is there anyone else you need me to call? I'm sure you'll need someone to drive you home, unless you want to fly."

"You can drive me," Garvin said.

"No. It's over between us, Garvin. I told you that already. I'm staying here. I hope you recover quickly and can get back to work soon. But that's it. We're done. I'll check back tomorrow and see if there is anything else you need before they spring you." Jolene started for the door.

"Jolene, please, don't go. I need you," pleaded Garvin. She stopped and turned to face him.

"Good-bye Garvin," she said, before turning back and walking out the door.

Astrid's arm throbbed with pain. Luckily, the bleeding had stopped. She drove like a madwoman, not sure where she was heading. She only knew she had to get out of there before the police found her. Of course, Jolene would tell them who she was, and where she lived. She needed to figure out a plan. She couldn't return to her apartment in New York. She was now on the run. *Damn Jolene! This whole plan had turned to shit! How did it get so out of control?* She wondered. Astrid didn't even know if Garvin was dead or alive. She could be wanted for murder! "Damn, damn, damn!" she yelled. What the hell was she going to do? Flashing red lights coming at her caused a moment of panic, before the ambulance roared by her.

"Oh my God. I thought that was the cops," she said shakily. "Get a grip. You need to think," she told herself. Pressing on the gas, she flew down the road, barely able to see in the rain. She knew the roads were slick. With no street lights, they were dark. Astrid prayed she wouldn't get into an accident, and barely navigated another sharp downhill turn, cursing Jolene, Garvin, the rain, roads and the entire state of Virginia. "Just get me out of here!" she yelled. She noticed it too late. A large brown dog with white paws was in the middle of the road.

"Holy shit! That can't be Jolene's dog!" Astrid stared, mouth gaping. In a flash, the dog jumped on the hood of the car, teeth bared, snarling and barking. She jerked the wheel to the right. The car ran off the side of the road. Astrid screamed as the car slid in the rain, spinning out of control. The car flipped over a guardrail, rolling and bouncing down a ravine until it landed upside down in the rocky creek below. The force of the impact was devastating. Steam rose from the engine. The only sound was the rain beating down on the car as the night engulfed the wreck. The dog, so vivid for Astrid, stood watching from the top of the hill. Then he slowly dissolved into the mist.

CHAPTER EIGHTEEN

Jolene opened the back door and stared at the kitchen.
Muddy bootprints were everywhere. Torn wrappings from the
trauma bandages and IV littered the floor, some mingled with
Garvin's blood. She glanced around and saw a bullet hole in the
wall. The place looked like…a crime scene. *Go figure,* she thought.
A writer of murder mysteries has a real-life crime scene right in
her own home. *You can't make this shit up.* Sighing, she decided she
couldn't deal with cleaning right now. *I'll deal with this in the
morning.*

Walking into the living room, she heard Gunner bark.
Startled, Jolene looked around. Gunner was locked in the
bathroom. Caught in the chaos of the shooting, dealing with the
police and going to the hospital, she had totally forgotten about
Gunner. The cops must have shut him in the bedroom to keep him
out of the kitchen.

"I'm so sorry," she knelt and hugged the big dog. "Come
on, I'm sure you need to go outside." Gunner wasted no time
rushing to the door, Jolene hustling to keep up. The rain had
stopped. The dark skies were clear. Jolene followed the big dog
outside, watching as he relieved himself in the field next to the
house. She felt the tension of the night start to fade as Gunner
explored the field, sniffing out bunnies. She let him play for a
while, before calling him back to the house. Still not wanting to
face the mess in the kitchen, and all the memories of the night, she
led Gunner to the porch. Plopping onto the porch swing, Gunner
lying on the porch next to her, she finally allowed her mind to
wander. What a night. Slowly swinging back and forth, she
thought about what had happened. She knew there was a chance

of Garvin showing up. Marni had warned her about that. "Marni! Oh my God. I'll have to call her and fill her in." Jolene groaned. Marni would also have to wait until tomorrow.

Her thoughts turned to Astrid. *What was she doing here? And where was she now?* She suddenly felt exposed. What if Astrid returned? Jolene tried to convince herself that Astrid wouldn't be that stupid. She had shot Garvin. She had to know the cops were after her. There is no way she would come. But then again, she had appeared to be crazy. And crazy people didn't often behave the way you would expect.

"What a freaking nightmare," she said. "Why couldn't they just leave me alone?" Gunner heard the car before she did, alerting her with a bark. She saw the lights coming up the driveway. She jumped to her feet, heart racing.

"Please don't be Astrid," she whispered. She held onto Gunner's collar, backing up against the wall, trying to hide in the darkness. As the car approached, she realized it wasn't a car. It was a truck. Lee's truck. She almost collapsed in relief.

"Come on Gunner," she said. Hurrying off the porch, she ran to the truck. She threw herself at Lee as he got out, hugging him tightly.

"Whoa!" he smiled, hugging her back. "I'm glad to see you, too. Is everything okay?"

"Now it is. I guess I wasn't prepared for what the kitchen looks like. It's like the whole thing was so surreal. Then I walk in the kitchen, and it's staring me in the face. I tell you what. It's one thing to write about this stuff, but it's another thing to experience it firsthand."

"I can imagine. I've been on several shootings, and even murder scenes as an EMT. It isn't easy. Especially when it's someone you know. You just have to distance yourself from the whole thing. Otherwise, you can't do this job. It will eat you up." Lee looked down at Jolene. "You ready to go in?" Jolene nodded.

"Yeah."

Together they entered the house. Lee looked around.

"You look exhausted. Why don't you go lie down for a bit? I'll take care of this."

"No, you don't have to do that. Let's just go in the other room. I don't even want to embrace this tonight." Jolene tried leading Lee into the other room.

"Just give me a few minutes. This won't take long, I promise." Lee held up a hand to stop her protests. "Go ahead, I'll be in shortly."

Seeing how futile arguing would be, Jolene gave up. "Thanks," she whispered, giving him another hug. Going to the refrigerator, she took out a couple of bottles of water. After handing one to Lee, she left the kitchen. With Gunner at her heels, went upstairs to lie down.

Jolene thought she was too wound up to sleep, but surprisingly she was sound asleep within minutes. Her dreams started out bizarrely, soon turning to nightmares. She dreamed Astrid and Garvin were chasing her through the woods. She could hear them taunting her, laughing at her attempts to get away. She ran until she came to a river, jumping in to get away from her pursuers. But, she found the river too strong, and started to drown. Jolene felt as though she was suffocating, thrashing in her sleep, until she finally woke with a yell. She sat up in bed, disoriented, bathed in sweat, heart pounding as she gasped for breath. The nightmare dissipated. Eventually, she calmed down. Gunner whined and jumped on the bed, licking her face. Jolene wrapped her arms around the dog, resting her head against his.

"Thank you. I'm so glad I have you," she said softly. She released Gunner when she heard someone coming up the stairs. In her disoriented state, she had totally forgotten Lee.

"Feeling better?" he asked, sitting next to her on the bed. "I checked on you a little while ago. You were out like a light."

"Yeah. Except for the weird ass dream. Actually, it was more of a nightmare. But I'm better now, thanks," she smiled.

"Good. Listen, are you sure you still want me to stay? I'll understand if you prefer to be alone."

"Are you kidding? Of course, I want you to stay. I need you, Lee. The last thing I want right now is to be alone. Please, stay."

"Well, since you insist," Lee smiled broadly. "Gunner, would you excuse us a moment?" Lee gently encouraged Gunner to get off the bed. With a sigh, the big dog went over to his bed and lay down. Lee then moved up next to Jolene, wrapping his arm around her. "That's better." Jolene smiled and leaned into Lee.

"Yes, it is." Turning her head, she looked into Lee's eyes, then her lips met his. Lee pulled her closer, kissing her back passionately. His hands traveled down her back, and she began to unbutton his shirt. Not needing any further persuasion, Lee removed first her top, then jeans. Jolene struggled with his jeans, but soon they were both naked. She felt his hardness against her. He hungrily licked and kissed her breasts, his tongue flicking over her nipples. Jolene moaned and arched her back. Grabbing his erection, she pulled him inside her, wrapping her legs around his back. Lee groaned and began pumping, the bed creaking with the rhythm. Jolene tightened her legs, pulling him deeper. Within minutes, she bucked wildly as the orgasm exploded over her. Lee came a second later, his rhythm faster and harder until he was spent and collapsed on top of her. Neither said anything at first. Lee rolled onto his side and gently stroked her face.

"Holy cow," was all he managed to say.

"I was thinking more like holy shit," laughed Jolene. "That was amazing."

Lee smiled, "Yes. It sure was. Come here." He lay on his back, pulling Jolene close to him. She snuggled up and rested her head on his shoulder. Lee gently stroked her back. Before long they were both fast asleep.

Lee woke first. It was two in the morning and ice cold in the room. Shivering, he pulled the blankets over them.

"Damn, it's freezing in here!" Jolene snuggled under the blankets. "How can it be so cold?"

"I don't know," Lee said slowly. "I guess I'll have to check the heating system in the morning." Without warning, Gunner jumped up, startling both Lee and Jolene. He stared up at the ceiling, growling and barking.

"What the hell?" Lee asked. Jolene got out of bed, dressing quickly in the cold.

"Gunner, what is it?" she asked worriedly. Gunner stopped barking but kept up the low growl. He appeared to be following something neither one of them could see. Lee looked questioningly at Jolene as he too, got dressed.

A thumping started in the ceiling, soon followed by a scratching in the walls. Lee's eyes were wide.

"Is that what you've been hearing?" he shakily asked Jolene. She just nodded silently. "This isn't vermin."

"It will stop," Jolene whispered. Lee pulled Jolene to him, holding her tightly. "Lee…." He felt her body stiffen in his arms.

"What is it?" he asked quietly. Jolene was staring towards the bed. He looked at what she was staring at and felt his blood run cold. On the other side of the bed, in front of the wall, was a woman. Lee stared in disbelief. She was young, but looked worn out. She was dressed in a peasant style dress, like something from the Sixties. She looked at both of them for several seconds, then simply vanished. Lee and Jolene were both shaking.

"Oh my God," said Jolene unsteadily. "Please tell me you saw her."

"I can't believe it. Who was that?" he shook his head. "Let's go downstairs. Come on." Hurriedly, they made their way downstairs. Once outside the bedroom, they felt the temperature change. It was much warmer. They reached the bottom of the stairs, and stopped, looking back up towards the bedroom. The noise had grown in volume, combined with a shaking of the floor they could both feel.

"What the hell is it?" asked Lee.

"I don't know. But it's getting worse," Jolene replied. "It's never been this loud before. It's almost like it's really pissed off about something." They both looked at each other. "Oh boy. You don't think it's because of…?" She let the question hang in the air.

"No. It's probably coincidence," Lee answered. They both listened as the noise stopped as suddenly as it began. "Now what?"

"Hell if I know. I'll tell you one thing. I finally believe all the rumors about this place," replied Jolene.

"I hate to say it, but so do I. I can't get over that woman. Have you ever seen her before?" asked Lee.

"No. I've felt the cold spots and heard the noises. That is the first time I've actually seen a ghost. And I'll be perfectly happy to never see another one. I'm still freaked out."

"That makes two of us. Let's go in the kitchen." Gunner trotted down the stairs, no longer growling.

"Come on Gunner," Jolene said.

"You did a great job cleaning. Thank you so much!" Jolene kissed Lee as they entered the kitchen. Lee blushed.

"You're welcome. I couldn't let you look at blood first thing in the morning. It's not pleasant."

"You are incredibly sweet and thoughtful. I guess having mud colored flooring comes in handy for something. You can't see blood as easily. I can't believe you got it so clean. I'm going to make some hot tea. Would you like some? Or would you prefer something stronger?"

"Tea would be fine, thank you." Lee settled into one of the chairs at the table. "I can't get over what just happened. I don't know if you should stay here. Maybe it isn't safe."

Jolene sat across from Lee while she waited for the water to heat up. "Oh! I completely forgot! I have the psychic medium coming out tomorrow, well, today, to investigate. Janice, at the real estate office gave me his number. He said he would be here around ten this morning. I'm hoping he can get to the bottom of this. He should be able to tell me if I'm in any danger here. Do you want to stay and be here for the investigation?" Jolene hoped Lee would agree to stay. Even though she wanted answers, the thought of doing this on her own was making her nervous.

"Are you kidding? What's a psychic medium?" Lee asked dubiously.

"From what I'm told, he can talk to dead people. Or they talk to him or something. To be honest, I'm not totally sure how it works. Just what I've seen on TV. Please tell me you'll stay."

Lee sighed. "How do you know this guy is legit? He could

be a phony, and just out to take your money."

"Well, that part you don't have to worry about. He's not charging me anything. He told me he only investigates what he considers the worst cases. I guess he gets a lot of calls that aren't even paranormal. So, does this mean you'll be here?" Jolene pleaded.

"I guess so. That doesn't mean I believe in this guy, but I'll stay to make sure you're okay. I want to be sure he isn't here to rob you or anything."

"I'm sure he's not like that. But thanks for agreeing to stay. I feel better with you here." Jolene smiled, then got up to fix their teas. She carried the cups of tea to the table, handed one to Lee, then sat down again. She barely stifled a yawn. "I'm sorry. I think we should try and get some rest. I have a feeling we're going to need it. I hate to admit it, but I'm afraid to go back upstairs."

"I'm not crazy about the idea, either. But I agree, we should try and get some sleep." Arms around each other's waist, headed back upstairs.

CHAPTER NINETEEN

Drink in hand, Professor Rupert Kozmo checked his look in the mirror. He was wearing what he always wore on an investigation. Freshly pressed blue jeans and a black sweater which contrasted nicely with his short, grey hair. Every hair was perfectly in place. The outfit also showed off his slim build. He took a sip of his drink, pondering what was to come. As a psychic medium, he normally would get images or feelings prior to the actual investigation. Oftentimes, even days in advance. Today, he wasn't feeling much. All seemed to be quiet in the spirit world. He wondered if that meant there really wasn't anything paranormal at Jolene's house. He hoped this wouldn't be a huge waste of time. Finishing his drink, he took one last look in the mirror to be sure he hadn't missed anything. He turned to the dog watching him intently.

"Okay Seacrest. Let's go talk to some ghosts."

Gunner barked at the approaching car, waking Jolene and Lee. Scrambling out of bed, Jolene threw on her clothes, and bolted downstairs. She didn't bother to look in the mirror but ran her fingers through her hair in an attempt to look presentable. She reached the door just as Rupert parked his car. She took a deep breath in an attempt to calm her nerves. She felt Lee come up and stand behind her. They both watched Rupert get out of his car, then hold the door open. They stared in disbelief as a reddish brown Irish Terrier hopped out. The dog was wearing a plaid cap and bow tie. Rupert closed the door. The dog trotted daintily beside him as they approached the house. Rupert walked ramrod straight, yet fairly glided across the driveway. If Jolene didn't know better, she would assume he was a model. She could even envision Rupert and the dog in a magazine ad. Something British. All he needed was a horse, and a pipe.

"Oh…my…God…" Jolene tried hard not to laugh.

"Is that dog wearing a cap and tie?" Lee laughed.

"Stop it! Behave!" Jolene scolded him, choking back laughter.

"Jolene. Come on. There is no way this guy is for real," Lee said.

"Look, just be nice, okay?" she pleaded. Lee shook his head. Rupert reached the door, and Jolene let him inside. She was concerned at first how Gunner would react to the other dog. The two dogs sniffed each other. Jolene held her breath, hoping there wouldn't be a fight. She breathed a sigh of relief when Gunner walked back and laid down under the table. *Probably embarrassed to meet a dog dressed like that,* she thought. Though, she had to admit, it was pretty darn cute. The little terrier carried himself like he was special. Actually, he and Rupert both exuded confidence.

"Professor Kozmo, I'm Jolene. I'm so glad you came out," Jolene offered her hand. "And this is Lee." They all shook hands.

"This is Seacrest. He accompanies me everywhere," Rupert announced. "Now, as I told you on the phone, I don't want to know too much about what is going on, unless I specifically ask for more information. I prefer to let the spirits speak to me."

"Okay," Jolene said. Lee rolled his eyes. Rupert caught the look.

"I realize that not everyone believes in spirits, or psychic mediums. However, I know from experience ghosts exist. I've been doing this a long time. I know what they can do. This is not a lark. If there is anything in this house, Seacrest and I will find it.

But, if you prefer, we can leave," he chastised.

"I'm sorry," Jolene said. "Please, we didn't mean to insult you." She gave Lee a jab with her elbow.

"Yes, I'm sorry. Please, continue," Lee said, humbled. Rupert arrogantly pulled himself even straighter.

"Well. We shall see. Normally, I get images, or feelings about a place before I even start. This time, it wasn't until I was a couple of miles from here before I felt anything. It wasn't very strong then, but it is getting stronger now that I'm here. It's not a person. I'm getting an image of a necklace." Jolene and Lee exchanged a quick glance.

"A necklace?" she asked. Her hand immediately going to her throat, where the necklace lay hidden under her shirt.

"Yes. I don't know yet what it has to do with anything. Or even if has anything to do with this place. I'm just letting you know what is coming through so far," Rupert replied. "I'm feeling pulled towards the rest of the house. Would you prefer I lead the way?"

"Yes, of course. We'll follow you." Rupert glided into the living room, Seacrest at his heels. Jolene and Lee followed behind him. In the living room, he stopped. Seacrest walked to the closet door. He sniffed around the door, then slowly followed the wall to the small bathroom. Whining, he moved back along the wall. He stopped at the fireplace, before continuing back to the closet. After a final sniff, he returned to Rupert.

"What is it?" asked Jolene. "Did he find something? Is it a ghost? Is it dangerous?"

Rupert turned to Jolene. His expression was one of a professor about to reprimand a student who spoke out of turn.

"Do you always talk this much?" he inquired haughtily. "It would be much more helpful if you didn't speak unless I ask you to speak."

"There is no need to be rude," Lee bristled. "This is her house. I don't see why you can't answer her questions."

"Listen young man. I am perfectly aware who owns this house. I do believe I also told you earlier. If you do not want my help, Seacrest and I will leave. You can deal with what is here on your own."

"Lee, please. It's okay," she placed her hand on Lee's arm. "I'm sorry Professor. Please, continue." Lee glared at Rupert but said nothing.

"I need to go upstairs," he suddenly announced. Jolene and Lee exchanged glances again. Lee shrugged. They followed Rupert up the stairs.

Instead of going directly to Jolene's bedroom, Rupert went into the other room. Once again, Seacrest wandered the room, sniffing. With his cap and bow tie, he looked like a canine Sherlock Holmes. She wondered if he had a pipe. He seemed interested in the wall where Lee found the necklace. A chill went through Jolene. It was probably coincidence. It was an old house. Probably full of smells that Seacrest would find fascinating. Like dead mice. It doesn't mean the dog can find something paranormal.

"I'm getting the image of a woman," Rupert announced, breaking the quiet. Jolene and Lee quickly looked at each other, then back to Rupert. He appeared to be absorbed in a conversation only he could hear. "She's from another time. She's young, dressed in clothes from another era. She's not coming in clearly. I'm getting the feeling she's afraid of something." He slowly and quietly walked around the room, then stopped. "Is there an attic?" Jolene and Lee exchanged another glance.

"Yes. Do you need to go up there? It's not that safe," Jolene replied.

"I can feel something above us. If we can get in the attic, that would be helpful." Lee gave Jolene another look behind Rupert's back.   Jolene motioned to Lee to lower the ladder. Shaking his head, he complied.

"Be careful. The floor is not very strong. You can fall through if you're not careful." Rupert looked at Lee, raising an eyebrow.

"I'll watch my step."

They cautiously climbed the ladder and gathered in the attic. Seacrest stayed below. He stared keenly up at the opening.

"The woman is coming in stronger. I feel this room was a sanctuary for her. I still feel her fear, but it's not quite as strong." He walked closer to the far wall and stopped and turned to Jolene. "Did you find letters or papers in here?"

Startled, Jolene responded, "Yes, maybe, sort of. I mean, I found a piece of a letter. Actually, I found it in the room below here."

Rupert furrowed his brow, not speaking for several minutes. "The necklace. Did you also find it downstairs?" Lee and Jolene stared at Rupert. Neither had told him about finding the necklace.

"How did you know about the necklace?" Lee asked. It was Rupert's turn to roll his eyes.

"You're kidding, right?" he asked scornfully. "The necklace, and letters were up here. This is where she hid things that were important to her. Why? I don't know. Not yet anyway. Let's carry on and see what else we can find out."

Jolene opened her mouth to speak, thought better of it, and closed her mouth. She had no desire to be dressed down again. They returned to the second floor. Rupert wandered into the bedroom. Jolene silently mouthed a thank you to Lee for thinking of making the bed before he came downstairs. Lee smiled.

"I'm picking up another spirit," Rupert said. "This one appears to be male." He hesitated, then continued. "It's a male child's spirit. He's very shy, but playful. He's showing me a pond. He's chasing frogs. Oh my Lord. He's showing me he's in the water and he can't swim. He drowned. Oh how sad."

Jolene stared, mouth open. "There is a story that a young boy drowned on this property. That is amazing."

"There are several spirits around here. I think a number of people died on this land," Rupert said. "The woman is back. She's asking for help." Jolene gasped. Lee looked at her, puzzled.

"What is it?" he asked.

"It's just, well, I didn't tell you some of the things that happened to me. I've had phone calls where someone, a woman, said something like 'help me'. And another time, after I took a shower, on the shower door was written 'help me'. It's spooky."

"The woman just acknowledged that was her. You weren't imagining it," Rupert told them. After a pause, he continued, "Wait. She says she showed herself to you. Is this true?"

"Yes," Jolene said, looking over at Lee. "We both just saw her this morning." Rupert listened, then nodded.

"Let's go back downstairs. I feel we're missing something down there. Something she wants us to find."

Downstairs, Seacrest made a beeline to the closet next to the fireplace. He sniffed around, then started scratching at the door, whining. Finally, he sat and looked over at Rupert. Despite the feelings of anxiety and dread building in her, Jolene had to smile at the sight of the dog with his bow tie and cap. Rupert stood next to Seacrest. She could swear they were having a wordless conversation.

"Do you mind if we open the closet?" Rupert asked.

"Not at all," Jolene replied. She and Lee hovered close by, but stayed out of the way, giving Rupert and Seacrest room to work. Rupert opened the door. Jolene found she was holding her breath, half expecting something, or someone, to jump out. She found Lee's hand, gripping it tightly.

"I'm here," he said quietly, pulling her close.

"Thanks," she smiled up at him.

Seacrest trotted into the closet. They could hear him scratching at something. Gunner, who had been hanging back, joined him in the closet.

"Gunner, get out here, don't get in the way!"

"It's okay," Rupert said. "Animals can be very sensitive to paranormal activity. It's possible he senses something, too." Rupert looked into the closet. "They seem to be interested in the wall. The woman is back, but she's not telling me anything. She's just watching us." He furrowed his brow. "I really feel there is something here she wants us to find. We need to open the wall in here."

"WHAT? You can't be serious. You come in here, and now want to take out a wall?!" Lee was incensed.

"Lee..." Jolene started to speak.

"Jolene, this is bullshit. What next? Take down another wall? Destroy the house while you look for who knows what?" Lee said angrily.

Rupert turned, straightened to his full height and glared at Lee. "I will say this for the last time. I did not ask to come here. I was asked to come and help, if possible. I am used to non-believers, but I will not tolerate being treated so rudely. If you don't want my help, we will leave." Rupert whistled to the dog.

Seacrest reluctantly left the closet and stood next to Rupert.

"Lee, stop! It's my house, okay? I know you're just trying to protect me, but he's right. I called him, and I think we should respect his opinion. We can open up the wall inside the closet, but, if there is nothing there, that's it. I'm with Lee on this, I'm not going to destroy the place. We'll need to figure out what is going on without any further destruction." Jolene stared hard at Rupert, not sure what his reaction would be. She didn't want him to leave, but at the same time, she was beginning to think maybe Lee was right. Maybe this was a farce.

"Fine," Rupert snapped. "I don't think any more, *destruction*, will be needed. Now, if you don't mind, perhaps you can locate a saw or something to open this wall." Lee glared at Rupert.

"I have one in my truck." Without another word, he turned and left the room. There was an uncomfortable silence while they waited for Lee to return. Jolene knew they had pissed off Rupert. She didn't need to be psychic to feel the waves of anger pulsating off of him. Oh well. It is her house. She was fine standing her ground. Gunner, sensing the tension, came over and sat protectively next to Jolene. She absently stroked his ears, silently urging Lee to hurry. Finally, he re-entered the room, carrying several tools. Rupert stepped back as Lee brushed by him and entered the closet. He first studied the interior. Next, he started tapping on all the walls.

"It's the one to the right," Rupert told him.

"Yeah, I figured." Lee shone the light on the wall, noticing it wasn't a true wall. It was a sheet of plywood. Careful examination showed it was screwed in place. An uneasy feeling came over him. This was not what he was expecting to find. The interior of the closet was made with sheetrock. Why was one wall

136

plywood? It didn't make sense. Putting the saw down, he picked up the battery-operated driver.

"Can one of you hold the light for me, please?"

"Sure," Jolene said, squeezing in behind him.

"Thanks. Just shine at the top corner. I'll start there." Lee struggled a bit in the tight space, but eventually had all the screws out. "Okay, step back, please. Let me get this out of the way." Jolene backed out of the closet, still holding the light. Lee wrestled with the plywood, cursing a bit, until it gave way. Carefully, he pulled it out, setting it against the other wall.

"Hand me the light, please." Jolene silently handed over the light, holding her breath. Her heart was pounding. What if they found something hidden away? What if they didn't? She wasn't sure which would be better. If there was nothing there, she felt Lee and Rupert might get into an argument. She could envision Rupert stomping off in a huff. Then she would never find out what was haunting the house, or why. On the other hand, if they found something, it still might not explain everything. She realized she was shaking. She glanced at Rupert, but his expression was unreadable.

"Holy shit!" Lee shouted.

"What is it?!" Jolene moved forward.

"I do believe he found her," Rupert said calmly. Jolene heard him, but didn't register what he said. She was already standing behind Lee, who was staring into the open space. Lee moved over slightly. She could finally see what he was looking at. Her jaw dropped. Her hand flew to her cover her mouth. She started shaking violently, feeling faint. Lee put his arm around her, supporting her.

"Oh my God, oh my God, oh my God!" Tears filled her eyes. "Oh my God." Her brain could barely process what she was seeing. The space was dark, except for the light Lee shone into the room. In the light, on the floor, lay two skeletons. A woman, and a dog.

"Come on. You need to sit down," Lee said as he gently led her out of the tight space and guided her to the couch. Jolene was stunned. She looked up at Rupert.

"You knew. You knew what we would find, didn't you?" Jolene stared at Rupert. He nodded, sitting down next to her on the couch.

"When we were upstairs, she showed me an image. I was fairly certain we would find her in the house," he said gently. "The images aren't always clear. All I could tell is that she was in a tight, dark area. It could just as easily have been a crawlspace. That would have made more sense. I had to trust Seacrest on this one. He was the one who found her." Seacrest jumped up and sat next to Rupert. Gunner headed to the closet.

"Gunner, no! Come here," Jolene called. Gunner hesitated, looked back towards the closet, then turned and walked over to Jolene. Lee stood nearby.

"I guess I owe you an apology," he said to Rupert. "As you can tell, I didn't believe any of this hocus pocus. After what we experienced this morning, I had to admit there are some things we don't understand. I felt and heard things I couldn't explain. Then, I saw a ghost. But that doesn't mean I believed you could talk to dead people. Now, I reckon anything is possible. I'm still a bit skeptical it was your dog that found her. Him and Gunner. But maybe you can talk to ghosts. Either way, I'm sorry for what I said earlier."

Rupert didn't respond right away. He sighed. "Apology accepted. All I ask is that you open your mind to the possibility. Once you do that, remember what happened here today. You may be surprised at what you believe. Jolene, are you okay?"

Jolene shook her head. "No, not really. I literally have skeletons in my closet." She turned to Rupert. "Did she show you what happened?"

"Yes. Do you want to hear?" he asked gently.

"How about I venture a guess. Her husband shot the dog, then used the dog as a lure to get her in the closet. She freaked out when she saw the dog. They got into a fight and he knocked her out. Then, he sealed up the closet, and left her to die."

Rupert looked surprised. "That's close enough. How did you know? Are you sure you aren't a psychic medium, too?"

"It's the book I was writing. Pretty much everything you said today, it happened in my book. It's funny, I was beginning to think someone was using me to write their story. It was almost like the book was writing itself. Now I guess I know why. I just can't believe all this." She pulled Gunner close and hugged him. "I am totally freaked out." Rupert patted her hand.

"She wanted to be found. All the other people that lived here, no one would help her. You were the only one. She felt connected to you. I feel there is something in your life that paralleled hers. I'm guessing it involved a man. That's why she left the necklace for you to find. May I see it?"

Jolene pulled the necklace from under her shirt and showed it to Rupert.

"It's beautiful," he said. "I think you'll find things much calmer and quieter now."

"Is she gone?" Jolene asked.

"Yes. The little boy is, too. She took him with her to the light. They are at peace." No one spoke, each absorbed in their own thoughts.

"I guess we need to notify the police," Lee said.

"Yeah, I guess you're right. Do we have to do it right now? I need time to adjust before they come back out here."

"We can wait a little bit. Whoever she is, she's been here a long time. Another couple of hours won't hurt." Lee sat on the arm of the couch, softly stroking her hair.

"Well, I guess my work is done. I'll leave you two alone. If you have any questions, or anything, please call me. I must say this has been quite an experience." He stood up. "I'll let myself out. You have my number if you need me. Come along Seacrest." Lee and Jolene watched as Rupert floated out of the room, Seacrest trotting proudly beside him.

"This has got to be one of the weirdest days of my life," Lee said.

"Same here." Jolene leaned her head back on the couch. They both jumped when Jolene's cell phone rang. It was Marni. Jolene answered.

"Jolene! Where the hell have you been? I've been sick with worry! Did you get my message about Garvin? He's on his way down there!"

"No, I didn't. But it's okay. You would not believe what has happened." Jolene smiled up at Lee. "Let me fill you in."

CHAPTER TWENTY

"So, how are you? Tell me the truth," Marni asked.

"I'm okay. Though I'm still coming to terms with everything that happened," Jolene said. "My head is still spinning."

"Look on the bright side. You now have firsthand experience with crime scenes," laughed Marni.

"You got that right. Oh my God. I called the cops out the day after Rupert left. You should have seen it. There were police cars everywhere! I mean, the woman has been dead for years! But, I guess they couldn't resist. How often do they get a call for a body in a wall?"

"Have you found out who she was yet? Or how she died?" Marni asked.

"I think they pretty much know. The Medical Examiner is trying to track down relatives to check DNA. They can try matching to a family member. It looks as though she died due to no food or water. It really was a horrible way to die. I told the police when the ME is done, I'd like the woman and dog to be buried together. It seemed right, you know?"

"That's very kind of you. I'm sure she will be happier. Have the paranormal events settled down?"

"Yes. Rupert was right about that. He said things would be calmer. He is a character. I wish I had thought to get a picture of him and Seacrest and send it to you. You would have died. But, I must say, he knows his stuff." Jolene smiled at the memory of Rupert and Seacrest doing the investigation.

"I heard Garvin is back at work. Has he contacted you at all? I still can't believe that shit. I'm so glad you're okay," Marni said.

"Yeah, it was pretty damn scary. No, he hasn't called. I made it crystal clear I never wanted to hear from him again. I think he's also a bit freaked out about Astrid. I told you they found her, right?"

"Yeah. You said her car was upside down in a creek or something. Good riddance, is what I think." Jolene could hear the anger in Marni's voice.

"Yeah. It was a couple of days before anyone found the car. I don't know, Marni. Even after everything, I didn't want it to end like this," Jolene replied wistfully. "It's just all so unnecessary and sad."

"You're too good. She stole Garvin from you, then tried to kill you. I'm sorry, but I'm not that charitable. It would have suited me fine if they both ended up in the creek."

Jolene sighed. "I know. But, it's over. Let's move on. At least now I can focus on the future."

"Does that future include Lee?"

"I sure hope so," laughed Jolene.

"Does it also include a new book? And yes, I'm getting antsy," laughed Marni.

"Yes. The book is coming. I think you'll really like this one, too. It should sound pretty familiar after everything that went on."

"I can't wait to read it. And Jolene, I'm so glad you're okay. I know what you went through was pretty horrible, but I can already tell that you're on the mend. You sound so much better. I was really worried about you, you know."

"I know. Thanks Marni. You're the best friend I could ever ask for. Well, I guess I better hang up. I have a book to finish," Jolene said, smiling.

"Take care of yourself. I'll be waiting on that book. I'll also be waiting on a wedding invite," laughed Marni.

"Marni! You are bad! We just started dating. Let's not rush things!" Jolene was glad Marni couldn't see her blushing.

"Whatever. I'll still be waiting. I'll talk to you later. Bye!"

"Okay, bye," Jolene responded. Hanging up the phone, she found herself smiling. Wedding? Who knows. Maybe. She wasn't kidding when she told Marni she wasn't rushing things. She would take it one day at a time. She was just glad to be able to live her life in peace. The thought of Lee made her smile. It was such a joy to have someone who truly cared about her. She felt as though she had it all. A nice, caring boyfriend, house, farm, and dog. The only thing she needed now was to finish the book. Marni was getting impatient. She had to get it done. She sat at the table, staring at the blank page. Finally, she knew where to begin, and how this story would play out. She began to type.

THE SECRET OF THE BLOODSTONE NECKLACE

The old house sat vacant, lonely, year after year. The once bright white paint weathered to grey. Mice, seeking safety and food, worked their way inside, taking up residence in the walls and attic. Black snakes, searching for a meal, followed the mice. The air inside was stale. A sense of desolation and sadness filled the house. Outside, the grass grew tall, providing cover for the quail and other creatures. The seasons passed. Still the house sat empty. Waiting. It knew someday, the right person would come along. Someone who would uncover the secrets the old house held. Someone who would set it free. Until then, the house, and its secrets, would wait.

She pulled into the nearly overgrown gravel driveway, parking behind the house. It looked even more decrepit than she remembered. It looked abandoned and the sadness was palpable. The weatherbeaten sign dangled above the door. She could barely read the faded letters: BLOODSTONE MANOR, est 1901. Not for the first time, she wondered if buying it had been the right thing to do. There were thousands of houses out there that were in far better shape than this one. What was it about this one that had drawn her to it? Even now, standing in the driveway, she could feel it reaching out to her. It was almost like the house was calling to her. Like it had something to say, a story to tell. Well, she was a writer, after all. Picking up her bags, she headed into the house. Let the story begin...

ABOUT THE AUTHOR

Susan M. Viemeister has long been fascinated by things that go bump in the night. She realizes things aren't always as they appear to be, which she brings to life in a captivating and thrilling way in her novels. Living in a Victorian farm house in rural Virginia, where things really do go bump in the night, has reinforced this belief. From the time she was a small child, telling ghost stories on dark, summer nights, to the present, Susan enjoys sharing these possibilities with her readers.

Currently at work on the next Parker Williams mystery, you can connect with Susan at her website: susanmviemeister.com or email susanmviemeister@gmail.com

Made in the USA
Columbia, SC
14 July 2019